NOT ON A
WHITE HORSE

NOT ON A WHITE HORSE

by Nancy Springer

ATHENEUM   1988   NEW YORK

Copyright © 1988 by Nancy Springer

All rights reserved. No part of this book may be reproduced
or transmitted in any form or by any means, electronic or
mechanical, including photocopying, recording, or by any
information storage and retrieval system, without permission
in writing from the publisher.

Atheneum
Macmillan Publishing Company
866 Third Avenue, New York, NY 10022
Collier Macmillan Canada, Inc.

Composition by Haddon Com-Com, Allentown, Pennsylvania
Printed and bound by Fairfield Graphics, Fairfield, Pennsylvania
Designed by Jean Krulis
First Edition

10 9 8 7 6 5 4 3 2 1

Library of Congress Cataloging-in-Publication Data

Springer, Nancy.
Not on a white horse.

SUMMARY: From the day twelve-year-old Rhiannon
spots a lost white Arabian gelding in the woods near her
small Pennsylvania mining town, her life finds a focus as
she learns to deal with family problems and decides the
direction her life will take.
1. Horses—Fiction. 2. Family problems—Fiction.
I. Title.
PZ7.S76846No 1988 [Fic] 87-3477
ISBN 0-689-31366-7

TO MOM, WHO SHOWED THE WAY.

NOT ON A
WHITE HORSE

ONE

"Lost, white Arabian gelding. Last seen wearing red halter and trailing lead rope, area Turkey Ridge Road. Reward. Phone 427-4936."

Rhiannon raised her eyes from the day-old newspaper and stared out the kitchen window at rows of plain-Jane, mine-town houses edging up a steep hill. Turkey Ridge Road was not far from where she lived. A white Arabian, loose around here somewhere? Amid the scrubby woods, the black slag heaps, the weedy strip sites? Rhiannon felt as stunned as if she had awakened one morning to find a unicorn eating the faded flowers off her bedroom curtains.

Dazed, she got up and wandered upstairs to the bathroom, where she combed her dark hair for no reason, looking blankly at her young face in the mirror. Smudges of yesterday's attempt at mascara showed under her brown eyes. She wet a washcloth

3

and scrubbed them off. Then she found herself in her bedroom, changing her jelly sandals for socks and jogging shoes. Before she knew she had made up her mind she was down the stairs and outside, letting the old wooden screen door slam behind her, running to the cinder block garage and looking at her bike.

She hadn't ridden it yet this summer. It was only the beginning of June, just a few days after school let out. . . . Well, maybe she hadn't ridden it last summer either. Girls her age, middle school age, mostly didn't ride bikes anymore, except for a few rich kids who had ten-speeds. Rhiannon had a bike with one speed, twenty-inch wheels, high handlebars, scratched pink paint and pink flowers on the banana seat: a little girl's bike, left over from the easy-money days before her father had been laid off, before he had started drinking too much. There would be no other bike for her, and this one's tires needed air. Rhiannon found a rag, rubbed off a thick coating of dust, and wheeled the pink embarrassment out. Walking, she took it down the sidewalk toward Zubrod's Amoco to use the air pump.

There was a rapt look on her face. Even if it meant riding her outgrown toy of a bike, she was going to find that white horse. Or at least see him. If it took her all summer.

Rhiannon got her mystic streak from her name, maybe. It was Welsh, and it meant "goddess of white horses." Her mother had chosen it out of a paperback book of names for the modern baby. Never mind that

Rhiannon was mostly Italian. In a town full of ethnic mixing, there was nothing so odd about the name Rhiannon DiAngelo. Anyway, the name suited her. She had always been crazy about horses, white or otherwise.

But there was not a chance in the world that she could ever have a horse of her own, or even have riding lessons. Not the way things were in Hoadley, not a chance of a chance. Nobody she knew had a horse.

"Hi, Ree!"

Her friend Lisa was hanging around the Amoco, maybe hoping some boy would buy her a Pepsi. Lisa looked pretty, as always. Narrow, beaded ribbons dangled from a clip in her reddish blond hair. "Hi," Rhiannon greeted her. "Want to go for a ride?"

Lisa stared at the bike with distaste wrinkling her freckled nose. "Oh, wow, you must be bored," she said.

"I just want to get out of here," Rhiannon said, though in fact she had been bored enough to read her grandmother's passed-along newspaper in the middle of the day, even the classified ads. Bored silly, and summer was just starting. "You coming?"

"Let's walk up Hoadley to the ThriftiDrug instead. I want to look at the mags." Wanted to hang out, Lisa meant. You wouldn't catch her on a bike. How gross.

"Nuh-uh. I'm riding back the mine road. Come on!"

"Aw, Ree—"

"Come *on!*"

Even though Lisa was a year older, which made her a teenager, thirteen, Rhiannon was taller and seemed older, and Lisa always did what Rhiannon said when Ree used that tone. Sighing, Lisa headed toward her house a few doors away to get her own bicycle, every bit as outgrown as Rhiannon's.

Ree filled her tires, listening to the dinging of the pump above the clang of tools inside the Amoco, the thudding rhythm of somebody's radio. Some young men were working on a car in there. Above the weeds and poison ivy straggling up the walls somebody had printed a few obscene words. The railroad tracks ran behind the place, then slantwise over the street, which ducked beneath them between narrow walls of redstone stained black with coal dust. On the black metal of the overpass somebody had spray painted, "Welcome to Nowhere."

Maybe Hoadley was *Nowhere,* but 27, where Ree and Lisa lived, wasn't even Hoadley. A place clinging to the edge of Hoadley like a tick to a dog, it didn't even have a name, just a number. There were others like it: Mine 33, Mine 20. Mine 27, long closed.

Lisa came back with her bike—her tires needed to be filled, too. Then the two of them started back the way Rhiannon had come, down the only street in 27.

Rhiannon's father was up on Kohut's porch roof, painting the house. Old Mr. Kohut couldn't afford to pay much, but it was a job for a few days; it gave Bob

DiAngelo something to do. Rhiannon yelled hi and waved at him as they passed, and he turned around. "Ree-*ann*-on!" he hollered. "Bring me a beer, wouldja?"

"Can't!" she called back over her shoulder.

His mother, Rhiannon's grandmother, was sitting out on her porch next door, and she waved. She would get him a beer. Aunt Linda was working in her yard a few houses farther along. Grandma Phillips was hanging wash.

Ree and Lisa puffed up a small hill, crested it, and swooped down past the remaining houses toward the yellow metal gate that kept cars out of the unpaved mine road. Off to one side Rhiannon heard the shouts of boys zooming their bikes up and down the crazy slopes of the "bony piles" of slag, cutting donuts and daring each other to risk the steeper paths, jumping ditches and popping wheelies. Her younger brother Shawn would be there, and he would come home for supper covered head to foot with black grime, the way Grandpap used to come home from the mines. The girls veered their bikes around the gate, and trees closed overhead. They left the shouts and the shabby row houses behind them.

It was like being in another world, or at least so it seemed to Ree. A hushed, cool, dim world. Leaves rustled softly. Saplings reached for light. Fallen trunks lay covered with moss and mushrooms. Ferns rippled down the banks of the black gravel road. It ran on the level below a steep hillside, and the girls pedaled their little bikes steadily through a silence broken only by the chirps of unseen chipmunks. Mountain laurel and hemlock crowded the road. Tall locust and maple cast a dense green shade.

"It's *creepy* in here," Lisa said.

"Shush," Ree told her, peering between the tree trunks to either side.

"Let's go back."

"Will you hush up? I'm looking for something."

"Like what?"

But Rhiannon would not tell her. A dream image of the white Arabian wafted through her mind like a wind through the woods, and somehow she could not share it with anyone.

On the hilltop far above their heads ran Turkey Ridge Road.

The deep shade lightened as they reached the end of the mine road. In an overgrown clearing stood what was left of the tipple, its timbers in a jumble, like spilled matchsticks. The girls took the sketchy road that looped around it and started back the way they had come.

"Thank goodness," Lisa sighed. "What is it with you, anyway?"

But Rhiannon was looking off through the woods downslope, toward an orange gleam where Trout Creek ran. Orange, because mine runoff had turned all the rocks of the mountain stream the color of sulphur, and the water itself had an acid taste. No trout in Trout Creek anymore. But a lost horse would have to drink somewhere.

There was even a hint of a trail.

Abruptly she stopped, let her bike fall into the weeds that edged the road, and headed down the rocks on foot. Lisa followed.

"You goof, watch for snakes! You hunting for fossils or what?" Kids sometimes found fossils among the shale bared by creeks or strip sites.

"Would you shut up?" Rhiannon exclaimed between her teeth. "You'll scare him!"

Lisa demanded, "Scare who?"

A grouse flew up with a rush from nearly under their feet, making both of them jump and scream, then laugh. At once a crashing sound rattled the woods. Something big was moving in the brush. Rhiannon gasped and pointed at a glimpse of white—

And a doe deer bounded away, its white tail and backside bobbing like a ghost through the maple saplings.

Rhiannon started to giggle.

"What is *with* you?" Lisa asked again.

Still laughing, giving up on shushing anyone, Ree ran down what was left of the trail to the creek.

It stretched maybe fifty feet wide in places, but rocky and shallow. Rhiannon fell silent and looked up and down it as far as she could see, then started walking along the brushy shore. She fought her way

9

through tall weeds and blackberry brambles for quite a while, not sure why. Certainly nothing as big as a white horse was hiding in them.

"I'm getting all scratched up," Lisa complained.

"So go on back."

"So you can call me chicken? No way. You better tell me what you're looking for!"

The creek curved, and at the bend lay a mud and gravel flat covered with deer tracks and the handlike prints of raccoons. Both girls stepped out on it, glad to get away from the weeds for a while. Rhiannon bent over and scratched at the fresh mosquito bites on her bare legs. Then she stared.

Nearly under her own feet was the deep, crescent print of a horse's unshod hoof.

Instantly forgetting bug bites and briar scratches, she dropped to one knee, fingering the hoofprint. There were two more at the edge of the weedy bank. She looked at them, a dreamy smile on her face.

"Aw, jeez!" Lisa wailed in protest. "I should've knowed it would be a horse!"

As far as Lisa was concerned, horses were for babies and elementary school kids, the My Little Pony crowd.

"Aw, maaan! I am going home!" Lisa turned and stomped away, heading back toward her bike. After a moment Rhainnon followed. The horse tracks were probably a couple of days old. They might even have been left by a different horse, by someone riding along the creek—though Ree had never seen anyone riding down there. In her heart she felt warmly certain that she had just touched the hoofprint of a white Arabian. She felt convinced in a way the newspaper had not been able to convince her: The horse was real.

In absorbed silence she rode home, feeling her dreams form into plans, letting Lisa scold at her. All the way to her backyard she hardly said a word. Then she said one, but it was only an automatic, "Bye," to her friend. Lisa went home, out of breath and grumbling, and Rhiannon put away her bike and let herself into the house.

There was nobody home. She had known there would not be anyone. Her father was still at his painting job, her brother Shawn was still out bike riding with his friends. Rhiannon's mother was at work. Since the steel mills had closed and Bob was unemployed, Bonnie DiAngelo was working two jobs at once, shift work at the shirt factory and part time at the local convenience store. Women's work, the jobs didn't pay well, and there was never enough money for anything. Rhiannon's older sister, Deirdre, earned a little bit baby-sitting, but not many people hired sitters. That was what grandmothers were for, sitting kids. Anyway, as far as Ree could see, Deirdre was more interested in boys than in working. Lord only knew where she was, but she was never home.

Rhiannon flopped down on the sofa in the empty house. If she wanted company she could go to Lisa's place, or to her Grandma DiAngelo's, or to her Grandma Phillips's a few houses beyond, or her Aunt Linda's, or any of a dozen places right in 27. But she didn't want company. She wanted to think about the white horse.

She wanted to call the number in the newspaper ad, but felt shy. A hoofprint was not much to go on.

After a few minutes she got up, went to where the paper lay on the kitchen table, and found the ad again. She ought to clip it—but that would leave a hole in the paper, and someone would ask questions. Rhiannon felt very private about the Arabian, as if the search was her secret, a matter for her and her dreams alone. Letting Lisa know as much as she did had been a mistake. Rhiannon stared at the ad, then went and found paper and a Bic pen left over from school. She copied the advertisement, the whole thing, then double-checked it, especially the phone number, and put the folded paper in her room, in her junk drawer where no one would bother it.

After a while Rhiannon turned on the TV and watched "Scooby Doo," then the local news, "Wheel of Fortune" and a "M*A*S*H" rerun. Deirdre came in from a day of swimming and hanging around at the community pool, watched the lottery drawing, made herself a bologna sandwich, changed into her tightest jeans and went out to hang around again at the drugstore or the pizza shack. Rhiannon kept watching TV. She had no interest in talking with Dee. Just because her older sister made a little baby-sitting money, she got to go to the pool and hope the blond hunk of a lifeguard would notice her. Big whoop.

Shawn came in, scuffing off his filthy sneakers and leaving them on the plastic mat by the door, as he had been taught. At once he started poking around in the refrigerator, looking for cold macaroni and cheese or cold baked beans, his favorites. Rhiannon turned off the tube and wandered out to talk with him.

"Better go wash first," she told him, "or you'll leave dirt all over everything and Mom'll come after you."

"I *am!*" Shawn snapped even though he plainly was not. Ree scowled. He thought she was being the snotty big sister. Well, she would be, then.

"And use soap!" she ordered.

"I *will!*"

"Might as well just go ahead and take a shower. Change your clothes and put the dirty ones in the laundry, not on the floor!"

"Aw, *maaan!*"

By the time Shawn came down, mostly clean, Rhiannon had found herself something for supper and felt friendly. She had even put out a plate and some cold spaghetti for Shawn. He ate hungrily, holding his fork like a shovel, and she watched.

"You ride bikes all day?" she asked after a while.

"Pretty much."

"Ever see any horses around here?"

"Nuh-uh." Shawn gave her the sharp look of a smart ten-year-old. "How come?"

"I mean, you ever see anybody horseback riding, like, down in the woods?"

"Why would I?"

Ree sighed, stifling an urge to strangle him. "I heard somebody up on the ridge has a horse."

"Oh, yeah." Shawn turned back to his food. "I knew that."

He would say he knew whether he knew or not, and it was no use asking any questions. He might make up the answers. Rhiannon stared past him, out the window where Hoadley was casting long shadows. Who could have a horse? She would never have the money to own a horse or anything else nice. A few lucky kids had newspaper routes and always had money. But there were no other jobs. Nobody paid to have lawns mowed, or if they did, grown men did it. Grown men were even working as supermarket baggers and restaurant busboys. When Deirdre got her working papers in a year, there would be few jobs for her, either, no matter what courses she took at Vo-Tech. People said things were better down toward Harrisburg—

The screen door slammed, and Shawn was gone while she was still thinking, leaving his dirty plate on the table for her to rinse. She put the dishes in the sink and went back outside herself. No one would wonder where she was. Her father would be painting until dark, and Bonnie DiAngelo had worked seven

14

to three at the shirt factory and was now working the supper rush at the Kwik-Shopper, serving up gasoline and hot dogs. The kids were expected to take care of themselves.

In the cool of the evening, Rhiannon pedaled back down to the mine road and cruised the length of it. Everything seemed very quiet, even the birds, and the slantwise light made the leaves shine like gold. Ree decided that she liked this place, even though kids told stories about ghosts and tramps and rapists back here. She saw several dim trails leading down to the creek. Deer trails, maybe. Up the road from her, at a distance, a deer leaped across, its summer coat as bright as polished copper.

Rhiannon left her bike and went down to the creek. She walked along it until the sun was down and the light began to fail, until she was far past the mine, but she did not see the white horse or any more hoofprints. Coming back, she splashed through the water in her hurry, soaking her feet. It was after dark when she got home, but her father did not notice. Slumped in front of the TV, drinking yet another beer, turning his steelworker's muscle into flab, he stared out from under black brows without seeing. Her mother was too tired to do more than look up and nod.

"How was work, Mom?" Ree asked, even though she knew the answer.

"Awful. My feet ache so, I could scream. What did you have for supper?"

"Sandwich."

"Nothing else? Have some fruit, then. An apple."

Rhiannon was tired of apples, but she had learned not to say so. Little things could throw her mother into a tantrum when she had just put in twelve or thirteen hours of work. Ree got a big dill pickle instead and sat across from her mother.

"Did you do anything around the house today?"

Ree shook her head. The trouble was, she never knew what she was supposed to do. She was afraid if she just did what came to hand she would end up doing it all, and Deirdre and Shawn should do some too. And though nobody said it, her father wasn't much use around the house, either.

"Honey, I don't have time or energy to be always telling you and telling you. Put in a load of laundry tomorrow, at least. Underwear or something."

"Okay."

"I can't do it all myself," Bonnie muttered as if trying to excuse herself or convince herself. "The place is such a dump since I've been working." She rubbed her face with her hands.

Rhiannon looked at her mother and noticed the lines around her eyes and lips without realizing that Bonnie used to be pretty. Blond Bonnie who had given her daughter the sort of special name she had always wanted for herself.

"I'll do the dishes tomorrow," Ree said reluctantly.

"Good. I'm going to bed." Bonnie pulled herself along by the handrail as she went up the stairs.

Rhiannon headed toward bed herself, and got out the old windup alarm clock she used for school mornings. She wound it, set the time, and set the alarm to go off early. Very early. Four in the morning. She had a feeling that the time to see a certain white horse might be at dawn or dusk. It might bed down during the day in the summer heat, like the wild animals. Though you would think a person would be able to see it anyway. Maybe it just wasn't there at all. It could be in the next county by now. In fact, she told herself, it probably was.

But her dreams were not listening to her. She went to sleep with the image of the white Arabian running at a floating gallop through the rivers and forests of her mind.

Nobody was awake when she slipped out of the house in the morning. A mist was rising from Trout Creek, wisping up between shadowy hills and trees, feathering into the brighter dawn gray of the sky. The whole world seemed as silent as the mist. There were no cars on 27 Street, no people. The houses stood as darkly as the hills, and the narrow road into the woods, behind its metal gate, looked as black as a mine shaft. The little pink bike swished through the hush as Rhiannon swooped down the empty street toward it.

Something white moved, floating like the mist, and the Arabian stood there on the old mine road.

White as an angel in the dark woods he stood, beneath the gray-green hemlocks, swan white against the black gravel of the road, so white he made Rhiannon's heart ache. And the proud lift of his head as he saw her, the flash of dark eyes and flex of his fine neck made her breath catch in her throat. She was so stunned when she saw him there that she didn't know what to do. Her bike hurtled toward him, and in the next instant he was gone like a wild bird. She caught a glimpse of long mane and flying tail, and then there was only the soft drumming of hooves somewhere beneath the trees. Then silence.

 TWO

When Rhiannon got back to her house around mid-morning, after hours of hiking and riding and calling to a white horse that seemed to have vanished like a ghost, she found Lisa sitting on the worn wooden steps of her back stoop.

"White Arabian," Lisa said in mocking tones. "I should've knowed."

In no mood to reply, Rhiannon glared at her, then went and put away her bike. When she came out of the garage, Lisa hadn't moved.

"That newspaper ad, right? White Arabian, right? You *really* think you're gonna find him?"

The scorn in Lisa's voice stung Rhiannon into answering. "I saw him!"

For one off-guard moment Lisa let herself be impressed, and her face showed it. But she recovered quickly. "Well, so what?" she countered. "They won't give you no reward just for seeing him."

Rhiannon walked up to her friend and stared. She had not been thinking at all about the reward. It was the white horse itself that was calling to her. She remembered his high-headed grace as he stood behind the gate—no, *stood* was the wrong word. Danced. Or lit, like a butterfly, and then took off again. So white. Remembering, she forgot the long, hot morning of hunting after him, and she smiled.

"So how are you gonna catch him?" Lisa wanted to know.

Ignoring her, Rhiannon trudged past her, up the steps and into the house, closing the door behind her. After making sure she was alone, she got her copy of the newspaper ad out of her junk drawer and went to the phone.

Her finger was not quite steady as she dialed the numbers. Three rings, four, five . . . Good, maybe nobody was home. . . .

"Hello?" A woman answered, sounding like somebody's friendly aunt.

"Hi, I saw your horse."

"What? Oh, the one that ran away? Is that what you mean?"

A slight change of tone in the friendly voice told Rhiannon that the woman knew she was speaking to a child. Ree flushed and started to mumble.

"You know, the ad in the newspaper, white Arabian—"

"Right, honey. You saw him? Where?"

The image of the white horse in her mind made Rhiannon happy and calm. She spoke clearly. "Down at the end of 27, just beyond the yellow gate. Then he ran away into the woods."

"Yes, he's good at that." The woman sounded wry but still warm. "When was this? Just now?"

"No, you know, this morning." Ree started to mumble again, realizing she should have called at once. "You know, early."

"Oh. Well, Chickie's not here right now, anyway," said the woman in a kindly way. "He's working over at Black Lick today. You see that Arab again, you call, okay? You can call as early as you like." The woman said good-bye and hung up.

Rhiannon went out in a daze and sat on the back stoop, where Lisa was still waiting to pester her.

"I phoned."

"So what did they say?"

"Chickie wasn't home."

"Chickie who?"

Ree shrugged, but she wished she knew. It sounded as if the people might have more than one horse! Who could they be?

"So what else did they say?"

"Nothing." Rhiannon scratched her mosquito-bitten shins, brushed away a tick climbing her leg, felt how sweaty she was and got up to go take a shower and hunt for ticks in her hair. But then she jumped down to the bottom of the steps in one leap and looked hard at her friend instead.

"You don't say anything to anybody about this, you hear?"

"What's the big secret?" Lisa protested. Her innocent look told Ree that Lisa was planning a laugh with her hang-out gang. Rhiannon lowered her dark brows into a fierce frown like her father's, the glare that she usually saved for Shawn.

"If you tell one single person, I'll tell the whole world about what you did with—"

"Okay, okay!" Lisa cut her off before she could say the name of the boy. "Sheesh!" She studied Rhiannon. "You gonna try and catch this so-called white horse, or what?"

"What do you mean, so-called?"

"Is it an albino? There's no such thing as a white horse if it ain't albino." Lisa wanted to save her pride by bickering.

"What's it to you?" Rhiannon grumped, but then she suddenly grinned. Those weeklong arguments about chestnut or sorrel, white or gray. . . . Lisa had been crazy about horses, too, until seventh grade, when she had decided to grow up and be crazy about boys instead.

"If it ain't albino, it's just a gray," Lisa argued.

Still smiling, Ree said, "Want to see for yourself? You're so nosy, it would serve you right if I made you help me look."

"No way!" But then Lisa pounced. "So you *are* going to keep looking!"

"Does Tarzan swing from trees?" Ree shot back, and she went into the house to take her shower.

She remembered to put some laundry in, afterward. She even did some dishes. But for the most part, that day and the next three days, she spent her time on the trails back in the woods. Her father finished painting the Kohut house, spent most of the money down at the Tipple Tavern, and bought several lottery tickets with the rest—none of them won. Bonnie's shift changed to three-to-eleven, and she worked the morning rush at the Kwik-Shopper. Deirdre turned her attentions to a dark-haired lifeguard named Keith. Shawn and his friends formed a club, arguing endlessly about rules. Rhiannon's Grandma Phillips complained that she never saw Ree anymore. But nobody else in the family noticed any change in her, even though she went to bed at nine every night so she could drag herself out of bed at dawn.

The fourth dawn, walking her bike around the metal gate and into the woods, she saw a white movement and a swish of long tail before the horse vanished into shadows. Hoofbeats sounded softly along the creek, echoing in the mist.

Rhiannon turned her bike around and pedaled hard back toward home. This time a sleepy male voice answered her on the phone.

"I saw your horse," she said. "Just now."

"Lord," the voice groaned, "you want my dad. He's out at the barn. Just a minute."

She waited. There was some hollering, maybe out of a window or door. After a while another voice came on the line, a man, and this one sounded awake. "Chickie Miller here. Hello!"

"I saw your horse," she said.

"This the same girl called before?"

"I . . . I guess so."

"You called before?"

"Yeah."

"Then you're the same girl." Chickie sounded cheerful, even at dawn. "Right? So where was he this time?"

"Same place, almost. Where the mine road starts."

"Just now?"

"Uh-huh. I mean, about ten minutes ago. Then he went down along the creek."

"Okay. Thanks." Chickie hung up.

Rhiannon pedaled her bike back to the mine road to see what would happen next.

She waited around the metal gate for what seemed like a very long time. Nobody came. "Blaargh," she muttered to herself, thoughts chasing through her mind. The man had somehow gotten there ahead of her—but there was no car parked at the gate. Maybe he wasn't coming at all. . . .

When she couldn't stand it any longer, she got on her bike and rode into the woods.

The sun was up and the mist was mostly gone. She

pedaled along, looking from side to side, without much hope of seeing or finding anything. The road curved around a boulder pile. Rhiannon rode around the bend—

Clopping toward her in the middle of the road was a sorrel horse under saddle, with a big man on its back. Rhiannon gasped and brought her bike to a skidding stop, but it was too late. Scared, the horse jumped violently to the side and back, its long head down and pointing toward her so that she saw the flash of white in its rolling eyes. With the next jump it tried to turn and run away, but the rider brought it straight again and to a halt. It stood puffing and snorting at Ree.

"Sorry!" Rhiannon exclaimed.

But the big man seemed not upset in the least. "Morning!" he said heartily.

It was, indeed, morning, and Ree nodded.

"Damn fool horses always spook at bikes," the man added just as happily.

His smile stretched all the way across his broad face. He looked German, Pennsylvania Dutch maybe, and he was big all over. Fat, but he was not sloppy fat, just chunky and egg-shaped, and his arms bulging out of a tight T-shirt looked as thick as Rhiannon's legs. Something young about him made it hard for Ree to decide how old he was. Older than her parents, she guessed.

"Speaking of horses," he went on, "you seen a white one running loose down here?"

Rhiannon felt her mouth come open in an uncouth way. "Oh," she said.

"What say?"

"You must be Chickie Miller," said Ree. Though it hardly seemed possible, his smile stretched yet wider. His small eyes lit up. "You the girl been calling me!"

Ree nodded.

"What's your name?"

She told him.

"What say?"

She tried again. "Rhiannon." Then, seeing his smile fade into a puzzled look, she told him, "Ree!"

He frowned, struggling with the name, then gave up and smiled again. "Okay. Pleased to meet you. Tell me something. You sure it was that knuckle-headed horse of mine you seen?"

Rhiannon felt her mouth gape again. "Is there more than one white horse loose around here?"

Chickie grinned. "Not that I know."

"He had to be an Arabian, anyway," Rhiannon added firmly. "He was so beautiful."

"Well, I got to tell you, it beats me." Chickie turned away from her a moment to scan the brightening woods around him. The big sorrel he was sitting on gave a final snort, decided that Ree and her bike were harmless, and stretched out its neck to browse on leaves. "Thought he would be miles away by now," Chickie said. "Or dead."

"Dead!" Rhiannon's chest suddenly started to ache.

"Hit by a car, or caught on something by the halter, strangled or starved. He have the halter and lead rope on him when you seen him?"

Ree held her breath for a moment, trying to calm the pangs in her chest and think. The proud, delicate face, wide white forehead, dark eyes. . . . She didn't remember anything on the head. "I don't think so," she said.

"Must've ripped it off somehow."

"Will he be all right?" Rhiannon asked anxiously.

"Huh?" Chickie turned his attention back to the girl, studying her. He lifted a hand and scratched his scalp through scrubby hair the color of peanut shells. "Well, yeah, he might be, if he got rid of the halter. There's no shoes on him. I let 'em go barefoot as much as I can. Farrier's horses ain't got no shoes." Chickie laughed at his own joke. His teeth were crooked and stained, giving his grin an impish look. Rhiannon stood, not understanding, but glad that the tight feeling was leaving her chest.

"So he'll be all right?" she insisted, and Chickie stopped laughing.

"No telling for sure, kid. Uh, Ree. But he's been okay so far, ain't he?" The big man scanned Rhiannon the way he had scanned the woods. "You up this early every morning?" he asked.

"Nuh-uh. I mean, yes, because I've been looking for him."

"I thought. Nobody else seen him. You want to keep looking? It ain't that big of a reward."

Ree just nodded. She didn't care about the reward.

"How you going to catch him if you see him? He ain't even got a halter on. You know how to handle horses?"

Twice, back in the days when things had been better, Rhiannon's parents had bought her a pony ride. Led around a dusty ring, feet dangling, she had sat in a happy trance. Twice, starting the year she was eight and old enough to go by herself, she had waited for the truck that brought the ponies to the fireman's carnival and volunteered to spend all carnival evening leading them around. When there were no paying customers, she had scrambled into a saddle and tried to ride herself, but the tired little nags would not go for her. After two years the rules had changed, and she was no longer allowed to lead the plodding ponies. Aside from those times, she had never ridden a pony, let alone a horse.

"I used to lead the ponies sometimes at the fireman's carnival," she said.

The sorrel had carried Chickie in among the trees with its browsing. He urged it back onto the road and made it stand on the grassy hump in the center, where it could not reach anything to eat. The horse tried to lower its head for grass, came up against Chickie's tug on the reins, grew restless and started to paw. "Quit," he told it sharply, and the sorrel stood still. Rhiannon wanted to pat it, but she curled her hands and stood as still as the sorrel, watching Chickie. The big man, she saw, had looked away because he was trying not to smile, and Rhiannon blushed, feeling stupid. Leading ponies was not much like catching a runaway Arabian.

Chickie reached up and broke a twig, stuck it in his mouth and chewed on it. This seemed to help him face her again.

"Even if the numbicile don't run from you, he'll run from the bike," he pointed out.

"I leave the bike and hike around here sometimes," said Ree in a small voice.

"That so." Chickie threw his twig away. "Well, there's a better way. Tell you what. I got to go to work now, but you come up my place this evening, we'll go looking for that pea-brained horse."

Rhiannon felt her mouth try several times before words came out. "You live up on the ridge?" she said finally.

"That's right. You know where the junkyard is, and there's a lane angles down in the holler? Has a keep out sign by it."

Ree felt cold, and she took a step back. She had seen the sign many times. It said, Private. Get Out! This Means YOU, and the O of YOU was painted like a rifle target, with a red bull's-eye for a center. Nobody ever went down there.

Chickie saw the look on her face and laughed.

"One of my boys painted that years back," he said. "It keeps the dirt bikers and snowmobilers out. Don't want them spooking my horses."

Horses!

"It don't mean you, not really. You're welcome to come anytime. Come tonight after supper if you can. Well, I got to get to work." He flapped one big hand at her and turned the sorrel with the other.

"You work over in Black Lick?" Rhiannon asked, suddenly wanting to keep him there a moment longer. He gave her a puzzled look.

"Black Lick? No, that was last week. I got to shoe a barn in Salamander today."

He nudged the sorrel with his legs, and it walked away with a soft clop of unshod hooves. The leather of the western saddle squeaked in the same rhythm. Rhiannon stood listening and watching. Some way along the old mine road the horse and rider turned onto a faint trail that ran up the ridge, and Chickie raised one hand and waved at her before he ducked out of sight under the hemlock boughs.

Shoe a barn? Salamander was down by Salamander Creek somewhere, but what—

"Dumbhead," Rhiannon muttered to herself, "he's a, like, a blacksmith. He shoes horses."

THREE

"Lisa and Jarod sitting in a tree,
K - I - S - S - I - N - G!
First comes love, then comes marriage,
Then comes Lisa with a baby carriage!"

It was Lisa's little sister with a bunch of her third-grade friends, chanting as they ran away from Lisa's back stoop, and Lisa looked mad enough to kill. Rhiannon had to giggle. Jarod was the boy Lisa did things with that she didn't want anybody to know about. Though they used the shadow of the railroad embankment behind Lisa's house, not a tree. Rhiannon pedaled faster and rode past on her bike before Lisa saw her laughing.

Biking up Turkey Ridge Road would have been a hard pull even on a ten-speed. On the pink bike with its child-size tires it was worse. Rhiannon walked half the way, pushing the bike, and even so she was puffing when she finally came to Chickie Miller's driveway. Glad she had left herself plenty of time, she stood there by the junkyard as the evening sun flashed off smashed windshields and curves of chrome, catching her breath and staring at the blood-red bull's-eye on Chickie's keep-out sign.

The woman had sounded friendly. Chickie was really nice, she felt sure of it.

And there were horses. . . .

An evening breeze washed across the ridge's crest, swaying the trees and cooling her. Ree took a deep breath, got on her bike and coasted gently past the sign, down the gray gravel driveway that angled along the Trout Creek side of the ridge.

In a moment the crest of the ridge rose far above her head. Locust scrub hid the junkyard and crowded around her. Twisted, half-dead apple trees, the remains of an old hillside orchard, poked through the brush—sunlight caught on their crowns, though in the morning they would have been in shadow. Then sunlight showed ahead, and Rhiannon came out into Chickie's hollow.

Plain white frame farmhouse with an old refrigerator standing on the porch. Weathered, unpainted barn and sheds, chickens running loose, cats prowling. Old plow rusting in the weeds. Car up on blocks, old pickup farther down the hillside, clutter of farm debris around the sheds, pond in the bottom. All of this Rhiannon faced without seeing it, for her eyes were on the horses.

Acres of pasture full of them. A dozen horses, maybe more, all with their heads down, grazing. Pintos, Appaloosas, buckskins, grays, chestnuts, bays— nearly every color, and Rhiannon could not begin to tell the breeds, except for the bright Appies and a tiny palomino Shetland pony grazing among the others. There might be thoroughbreds, Arabians, maybe even Andalusians. A person who would have an Arabian might have anything. Ree's glance darted from one to the next. She could not concentrate on any of them or take them all in. Sunlight on their glossy flanks dazzled her far worse than sunlight off glass and chrome. A dark horse, brown or maybe bay, raised its head and nibbled a pinto affectionately on the withers. A chestnut nipped a gray, starting a game—several horses began to run. Rhiannon gazed, trying not even to blink.

Her legs, without her knowing it, had braked her bike and walked her down the lane almost to the farmhouse porch, but there they had stopped as if stuck, and there she stood, gawking.

"You really love horses, don't you, hon."

Ree jumped as if she had been pinched, for she had not heard anyone coming. But there stood Chickie's wife, big as life, right beside her.

The woman had to be Chickie's wife. She had the same broad smile as he did, though her chin, when she stopped smiling, lifted and jutted so that she resembled a Load Commander coal truck. Her bosom lifted and jutted like her chin. She was gray-haired, like Rhiannon's grandmothers, but she wore a plaid shirt and sacky jeans, and neither Grandma Phillips nor Grandma DiAngelo had ever worn slacks in their lives. They wore housedresses like a badge of honor. This woman might be younger, Ree judged. Or younger at heart.

"Oh, hi," Rhiannon managed to say. "Mrs. Miller?"

"That's right." Her voice sounded full of good humor, like Chickie's.

"I'm—my name is Rhiannon. Chickie said—" She stopped, doubtful, though it somehow seemed okay to call Mr. Miller by his first name. And Mrs. Miller didn't frown.

"Yes, he told me. Said he saw that look in your eyes. But he's not home yet. You want to meet the horses?" Without waiting for an answer, Mrs. Miller led the way down the lane that wound between barn and sheds to a wooden gate set in a fence made out of old black rubber mining belts. Rhiannon followed as if in a trance.

The big sorrel Chickie had been riding in the morning—that was Punky, Mrs. Miller said. Short for Punxatawny, where it came from. Quarter horse, mostly. A tall, dark bay named Cameron, a thoroughbred. Toby, the pinto, because his spot pattern made him a "tobiano." And Shiloh, and Rowdy, and a sort of brownish horse named Hoss. . . . Rhiannon's head swam. She could not keep them straight. There were other horses in a farther pasture beyond a thin strand of electric fence. Chickie liked to keep his geldings separate from his mares when he could, Mrs. Miller said. She pointed out some of the mares. Cat, a former cutting horse. Jingles—that was the pony, someone's outgrown Christmas gift. Leaping Lena was a rangy gray mare who liked to jump fences, but not under a rider. Tiffany, Butterscotch, Cricket . . .

The geldings drifted uphill toward the gate where Rhiannon was standing.

"They're not always so easy to bring in," Mrs. Miller remarked. "They know it's soon feeding time."

Long heads presented themselves to be rubbed. Rhiannon stroked cheeks, scratched foreheads. The geldings pushed each other out of the way to be near her—Mrs. Miller scolded them, but let Ree feed them handfuls of the long grass that grew in clumps outside the fence where the horses could not reach it. Mrs. Miller patted a few horses herself, then watched, smiling vaguely.

"Do you . . . do you *ride* them?" Rhiannon asked.

The woman snorted. "Me? Heavens, no. Chickie does, some, but not enough. No, they're mostly just big, overfed pets."

One of the geldings, Rhiannon could never remember afterward which one, stretched his neck out, put his nose next to her head, nibbled her hair and blew in her ear. Ree stood in ecstasy. Chickie's wife chuckled.

"See, they know you love them, dear. Now to me they're just big animals, and I wouldn't mistreat any animal. But there's a lot like you are just crazy about them. Good thing, or my husband would be out of a job."

There was a rattling sound as Chickie's Ford pickup truck came down the lane.

"Speak of angels," Mrs. Miller remarked.

Rhiannon did not get home until dark. Her mother was still at work, but her father came out of the TV room to meet her. He smelled of beer, and beads of beer dangled in his mustache. Bob DiAngelo had not shaved in a couple of days, so his face looked dark, shadowed. He had been working on somebody's car. Ree knew it by his grease-stained T-shirt and jeans and the black grime still on his hands even though he had washed them.

"Where the devil have you been?" he demanded, but she met the question with a radiant smile. Nothing, not even the hard sound in her father's voice, could take away her joy.

"Dad," she exclaimed, "I've been riding! Horseback riding!"

She was hardly seeing the frown on his face at all. Instead, she was seeing Chickie Miller's horses as they came in for their evening oats. She was watching them eat again, and answering Chickie's friendly questions. Chickie smelled of horse and sweat, she had noticed, and he walked bowlegged, like a cowboy. And he chewed straws, and spat. She liked him. Then she was standing with a brush in her hand, watching him halter the brown gelding named Hoss and tie him to a fence post near the barn.

"Don't use that body brush on his face," Chickie had said, and then he had ambled off to get a horse for himself.

Then Ree had groomed Hoss. Awed, more reverent than she had ever been in church, she had approached the horse, running the stiff bristles lightly over his shoulder. Hoss twitched as if trying to shake off a fly, and Rhiannon heard a chuckle as Chickie returned with the buckskin, Rowdy.

"Harder! You're tickling him."

Ree watched as Chickie groomed Rowdy and tried to do as he did. Hoss stood like a stump for her. But Chickie was done before she considered she was well started.

"That's good enough," he told her. "They keep themselves pretty clean, rolling in the pasture. Just brush where the saddle and bridle and cinch go." He came over and gave a few swipes to help her, whacking Hoss as if to awaken him—the brown horse had not even moved his ears. "These ain't show horses. You just groom before you ride to keep them from getting sores. And pick their feet."

Chickie pulled a hoof pick out of the jumble of

brushes and lead ropes he had brought in a cardboard box from the barn. He bent over and lifted Hoss's hooves one by one, showing Ree the correct way to use the pick. "Heel to toe," he said. "Always keep the point toward the toe, so if the horse moves, it don't jab in." Hoss was unshod, and there was nothing lodged in his hooves except a little manure. Chickie straightened with a grunt.

"Hardly a chance in a thousand of a barefoot, pastured horse catching thrush or picking up a stone," he admitted. "But I'm prejudiced. I just happen to think folks should handle their horses' feet every chance they get. It makes the critters more mannerly for the shoer. You see how I might happen to think that way?" He grinned at her.

"Sure," said Ree. "You ever been kicked?"

"Ever been . . ." Chickie looked for a moment as if he had choked on the straw in his mouth. Then he spat it out and said, "Honey, if I had a nickel for every time I've been kicked, I could pay somebody to paint the barn. Let's saddle up."

He put a western saddle and a split-ear bridle on Rowdy, then helped her saddle Hoss, showing her how to smooth the pad into place, how to wrap and tighten the cinch. Rowdy wore a curb bit, but Chickie put a soft rope bosal and rope reins on Hoss. At his nod Ree went to mount.

"Not that way," he told her as she grabbed the saddle horn. "You'll just pull it over. Hold onto a hunk of mane."

"Won't that hurt Hoss?" Ree protested, and Chickie laughed.

"Hoss? You'd have to throw a dart at him to make him take notice. Even a thin-skinned horse, it don't hurt. They don't have no feeling in the mane. Grab hold."

He gave her a boost into the saddle and shortened the stirrups to fit her. Then he made a knot in the rope reins at the length where he wanted her to hold them. "Now," he told her, "if you need to tell him to turn, you twist your hand the way you want to go, and you nudge with that same foot and leg." He gestured, demonstrating. "It don't take much. And if you need to stop, you squeeze and release, squeeze and release, easy, till he stops. You don't need to pull on him. The bosal cuts off his breathing, so you don't want to squeeze hard or long. Hoss is a real dead-head, and he'll just follow along behind Rowdy if you let him, and Rowdy is real quiet, too. And we ain't going no faster than a walk tonight. So just relax."

It all seemed like a wonderful dream. She nodded, afraid to speak, as if a spell might break. Chickie got onto Rowdy with a rolling, lithe motion like that of a bear crossing a log. The big man spat on the ground and led off, and as he had promised, Hoss followed.

It was a real ride, out in the country, a trail ride.

Down along the pasture fence, with some of the other horses running up to see them off, prancing alongside. Rowdy's head came up, but Hoss nodded along like a donkey, nose at the level of his chest. Ahead of Ree, Chickie's sweaty back swayed in time to Rowdy's walk. Tall weeds swished around the horses' knees—Ree and Chickie were riding through a sort of overgrown field, an old strip site. Then they left field and pasture behind, ducked under branches and entered the woods.

"Just let Hoss have his head," Chickie hollered over his shoulder at Ree, "and lean back. Don't hang on the reins."

The trail dove down along the side of the ridge, so steep and narrow that Rhiannon held her breath. She had never known that horses could go such a place. They walked along a lopsided ledge above a drop she hated to look at, then slithered down a rocky slope, almost on their haunches. Rowdy and Hoss followed the rugged trail calmly, noses down, and Ree sat on Hoss's back, feeling the bulging of his muscles and the strength of his movements as he carried her down a mountainside. She sat still and leaned back and tried not to get in his way. In front of her, Rowdy swished his tail and shook his head, sending mane flying. Chickie reached forward to swat something.

"Deer flies are out," he said. "Should've used fly spray."

The land was leveling out, and Ree straightened up. Though she did not know it, she was sitting relaxed and deep in her saddle. She had learned to trust her horse.

"Watch the grapevine," Chickie yelled as he went under it.

She ducked it as he had. Then she saw a tree trunk coming at her knee—Rhiannon tightened that leg against Hoss's side to scrape by it, and to her delight the horse moved over so that her knee passed it with inches to spare. She trusted the horse, but she was not just a passenger after all. She had just made Hoss do something.

The trail came out on the old mine road. Rhiannon felt startled to find herself in a familiar place, but in such a new way. Everything looked different. Chickie stopped Rowdy to look around, and Hoss stopped as well, and Rhiannon stared at hemlock and boulder, laurel and fern and orange creek rock as if she had never seen them before.

"Here, boy!" Chickie hollered to the woods, and then he gave a shrill whistle. He listened a moment, then rode on.

"You think he's going to come to you?" Rhiannon asked anxiously, and Chickie leaned to one side and spat.

"Not likely. Only had him a day before he run away. He don't know me good, but he might come to the horses if he's lonely. Here, boy!" Chickie hollered again.

Ree said, "Wouldn't he come if you called his name?" With a limberness she would not have expected of him, Chickie twisted around so that he could look straight back at her over his horse's rump. He was grinning.

"Horses ain't like dogs," he said. "Anyways, he don't have no name except some fool Arab word I can't hardly remember, let alone say."

She stared at him, and his grin broadened.

"You saw him. What would you call him if you had him?" he asked.

Ree hadn't thought about it, but she remembered that first dawn glimpse of the white Arabian, and the answer jumped out of her. "I'd call him Angel," she said.

Chickie stopped his horse, put his head back and laughed up at the sunset sky. "I like it!" he whooped. "Horse knocks me over, kicks me in the butt and runs away, and she says call him Angel! I like it!" He put his head down on Rowdy's neck and laughed some more, then looked up to see Ree scowling at him.

"Don't bite!" he yelled, then laughed some more, then finally sat up and stretched out one square hand toward her in apology. "I'm going to call him Angel. I like it, I really do. I call this horse Rowdy because he ain't, and I'll call that devil of a proud-cut gelding Angel."

They rode on, and every time Chickie called, "Yo, Angel!" he started to chuckle, until finally Rhiannon grinned because she had made him so happy. Anyway, she was happy enough to laugh herself. They rode the length of the old mine road, then went back the way they had come, and Chickie taught her how to lean forward and cling to the mane as the horses scrambled up the steep trail, and she didn't even care that they hadn't seen a sign of the Arabian.

"You come Sunday afternoon," Chickie told her after he helped her down from Hoss, "and me and Hoss'll give you a riding lesson, and pretty soon you'll be able to ride out yourself after that darlin' Angel." He gave Hoss a slap on the neck and began to whistle to himself off-key between his crooked teeth.

Rhiannon didn't want to leave. She helped unsaddle the horses, lugging her saddle to its sawhorse in the barn. It was a cow barn, but divided into makeshift box stalls, and the tack and grooming box were kept in one of those. The walls, which looked ramshackle from the outside, had been patched with plywood or whatever came to hand on the inside, making them look even junkier there, but snug. Rhiannon led Hoss back to the pasture gate and helped Chickie turn both horses out. Then she hung around a little longer, watching them. The light was nearly gone when she left, refusing Chickie's offer of a ride. It would take her only a few minutes to coast her bike down the hill and be home.

Where she came up against her father's angry scowl.

Ree could not seem to stop her smile, no matter how anyone frowned. "Me and Chickie," she was saying with joy but not much coherence, "and I rode a horse named Hoss, down the ridge and everything! And the next time we're going to use fly spray and go down by the creek. And—"

"Who the devil," her father interrupted, "is Chickie?"

Rhiannon blinked. "He's this man who has the horses, Dad. Up on Turkey Ridge Road. He's a, like, a horseshoer. He shoes horses for a living."

"Who is he? What's his last name?"

"Chickie *Miller.*"

"Don't know him," Bob DiAngelo muttered.

"He's real nice, Dad!"

"Siddown," her father ordered, and Rhiannon did, at the cluttered kitchen table where the DiAngelos ate, sewed, did homework and talked. Mr. DiAngelo sat across from her and leaned forward to stare at her. "How did you meet this Chickie?"

Ree lost her smile at last and started to mumble. "You know, down in the woods. Like, he was riding, and we started to talk about horses. . . ." She didn't want to tell her father about the white Arabian.

"What the hun were you doing down in the woods!"

Rhiannon stared at him in surprise. Since when did he care where she went? "Riding my bike!"

"Listen, Ree." Her father was still frowning, but he didn't look angry any more. He looked serious, which was worse. "I don't want to say anything bad

44

about anybody I don't even know. But did this guy try to lay a hand on you?"

Rhiannon's eyes widened in shock for a moment. Then she felt her joy fly apart into fury. She jumped to her feet. "For crying out loud, Dad!" she shouted. "I'm not like Deirdre!"

Bob DiAngelo was on his feet, too, and for a moment she thought he was going to slap her for what she had just said about her older sister. But she was outraged, and she kept shouting. "Is that why you were waiting for me? You thought I was out with some boy? But it doesn't matter where I go in the daytime!"

"Shut up!" Bob DiAngelo yelled at her, shoving his face into hers. "Shut up right now, or . . ." She could smell the beer on his breath, and she glimpsed his balled fists. She shut up.

"You're grounded," he told her. "Now get to bed."

FOUR

When Rhiannon came downstairs the next morning, after a restless night, her father was sitting at the kitchen table, looking as if he had just washed his face in cold water. He had shaved, and at this hour he was probably sober, Ree knew.

"How come you're home?" she said bitterly. "Watching me to make sure I don't sneak out and run around with boys, I'm such a bad, rotten kid?" It was the wrong way to start, and she knew it, but she was so angry she couldn't help herself. Her father scowled.

"You're grounded," he said heavily, "because you rode your bike home after dark, and you were wearing dark clothing, and you didn't have any sort of a light. That's stupid, and dangerous."

"That's not what you were thinking about," Rhiannon said, "and we both know it."

Bob DiAngelo glared at her, got up, and went out.

Ree spent the morning in front of the TV. So all right, she'd be grounded, she thought sourly, but she was not going to do a thing around the house. If she did, her mother might start to like having her there.

She did not know for how long she was grounded, and she knew the way the morning had started wouldn't help. And it was only three days until Sunday. If she couldn't go up for her riding lesson, she told herself, she was going to . . . well, run away. Or something. It was bad enough, not being able to go up to Chickie's again this evening.

Nothing had been said about the telephone. Ree decided to think she was allowed to use it. Around eleven, when she figured Lisa ought to be up, she phoned her, and they had a long talk. In interrupted bits, Ree told her the whole story.

"Did you meet the Miller boys?" Lisa exclaimed at one point. "I know them. They work down at the Amoco. They're really cute. Hank Miller—"

"Aw, Lisa, come off it!"

The screen door slammed behind Rhiannon. She thought it was Shawn coming home for his lunch, and paid no attention.

"Who cares about boys?" Ree went on. "This is *horses* I'm talking about."

"So tell me about the one you rode. What color was it?"

"Sort of brown." Ree started to laugh. "Chickie says nobody can figure out what color Hoss is. He's sort of speckled with white, like he might be part Appy. Except maybe he's some sort of roan. And he's buffed out like a sorrel below the knees, but he's got a black mane and tail."

"Sorrels are light, like a palomino," Lisa said scornfully.

"Anything that gets lighter below the knees is supposed to be a sorrel, Chickie says."

"So? What does he know?"

"Only had horses ever since he was a little kid, is all. Only been riding since he was two." Rhiannon sighed hugely at the thought of riding. "Crud. If he just would have been a woman, there wouldn't be any problem. My dad thinks he's a dirty old man."

"Well," said Lisa, "how do you know he ain't?"

"I can tell!" Rhiannon's voice rose. "Don't you think I know anything about people? Chickie's nice!"

"But what's he bothering with you for? Don't you think he's got better things to do?"

"We both love horses! Isn't that reason enough? He's going to teach me to ride." Rhiannon started to sniffle. "Lisa, if I can't get up there Sunday afternoon, I'm just going to die."

"Talk with your dad. Maybe you can work something out. Maybe he can, like, come with you."

Ree said, "It's no use trying to talk with my dad."

"Just try."

"It's no use, I tell you! Ever since he got laid off, all he ever does is drink beer and say shut up. You can tell when he's coming by the beer smell. I don't know how Mom stands him. He never does a thing to help out around the house, and then he yells at her when he runs out of clean clothes. And then he goes to the tavern. And when he comes home he'd as soon slap you as look at you, and you have to stay out of his way. And all because he lost his job! Mom should lose her jobs, both of them, and then she'd be able to hang around feeling sorry for herself and never do any housework."

"Omigod, Ree," said Lisa. "Did he ever really hit you?"

"Not so far, but he hit Dee, I know he did. She came in late, after I was in bed, and I heard him yelling and I heard him hit her. He put a big bruise on her face, and she didn't go out for a week. He doesn't really care about any of us kids, him or Mom, either, or she wouldn't let him act like that." Rhiannon found that she was about to cry, and she hung up abruptly.

Somebody was behind her. She turned around and saw her father standing by the back door with a stunned look on his face. Before she could say anything to him he turned away and walked out of the house.

"Dad!" No time for crying now. Ree ran after him to the door, scared. She had never seen her father look that way, as if he had just been shot and hadn't yet fallen. Dad, I didn't mean it, Dad, I didn't know you were there—but before she could shout the words, Bonnie DiAngelo came hurrying through the backyard with an armload of groceries, home briefly between jobs. Rhiannon's father walked behind the garage to avoid her and went away somewhere, out of sight, and Bonnie shouted at her daughter as soon as she saw her at the door.

"Ree! Come help me with these groceries. I'm going to be late, they want me back to help with the noon rush."

Rhiannon could not begin to explain to her mother what was happening. She carried groceries in from the car, put milk in the refrigerator and black-and-white cans of food away in the the cupboards. Generic peanut butter, generic beans, generic whatever. Was a zebra a generic horse, or was Hoss? No meat except chicken dogs. Bonnie came dashing down from a quick trip to the bathroom upstairs.

"Did you get it all? Did you do any laundry today?"

Nodding to the first question, shaking her head to the second, Rhiannon felt adrift, as if she was floating through a nightmare, with no control. Bonnie DiAngelo snatched her purse off the table, then looked again at her daughter.

"What's wrong, honey?"

Rhiannon wanted to grab her and cry on her shoulder. Instead, she said, "Nothing."

"What are you doing this afternoon? Do you want money to go swimming? I still have a little time. I could drop you off at the pool if you hurry and get your things."

Her mother was trying to be nice. And it seemed that her father hadn't told Bonnie that Rhiannon was grounded. Bewildered, Ree shook her head. "Thanks," she mumbled.

Bonnie looked hard at her. Then she said, "Call me at work if you need anything," and she ran for the car. Rhiannon watched the rusty old Chevy Citation roar up the alley.

A moment later she was out of the house, on her bike and heading up the street toward Lisa's place. Grounded or not, she was going to find her father.

Lisa was sitting on her front-porch swing. Ree sent her to get her bike. "And hurry up!"

"You're going to be in trouble! You running away or what?"

"Just come on!"

Lisa followed Ree as they pedaled up street toward Hoadley. "Where are we going?" she wanted to know. "I thought for a minute we were after that stupid horse again."

Rhiannon was in no mood to smile. "It's my dad," she said starkly. "He heard me talking to you on the phone."

Lisa gasped. "Oh, wow! What did he do?"

"He just looked really weird and walked out. We're going to check all the taverns till we find him."

Lisa put on her bike brakes so hard she left a black streak on the pavement. "No way!"

"Yes, we are." Rhiannon kept pedaling.

"Ree, we can't! We'll get killed!" But Ree showed no sign of slowing down, and Lisa tore after her.

The closest tavern, but not the only one within walking distance, was the Tipple. BEER * WINE * LIQUOR said the sign, and a picture of a loaded coal car sat on the crossbar of the T. The door hung open. Lisa wouldn't go in, but stood with one foot poised on a bicycle pedal, gawking into the dim room, as Rhiannon marched inside. The place was nearly deserted at this noon hour. Only a couple of burly men lounged at the bar, and the owner was washing ashtrays. Rhiannon did not like the way they were looking at her. She went straight to the bar and spoke to the man in the apron.

" 'Scuse me! Have you seen my father?"

The dish towel in his hand kept rubbing at the glass, and he didn't answer.

"My father! Bob DiAngelo."

"Oh." He shook his head. "Not today, I haven't." He stared after her as she hurried out.

"Next place," Ree said crisply to Lisa.

"Couldn't he be at a friend's or something?"

Or at Grandma DiAngelo's, or Aunt Linda's? Not likely. Her father didn't go to his family with his troubles. He went to drinking buddies and bartenders. Rhiannon kept pedaling.

There was a tavern on nearly every corner, a bar

across from a church and a boarded-up storefront. Signs glowed in the small, dusty tavern windows: Pabst, Coors, Bud Light. The places were all dim, and they all smelled of beer and smoke. Men stared at Ree in all of them. Her father wasn't in any of the half dozen she checked.

"Maybe somebody give him a ride someplace," Lisa offered.

At a loss, Rhiannon stopped her bike and bit her lower lip. Her father would not have gone much farther up Hoadley, walking. Where could he be?

Atop Hoadley fire hall a siren went off. Ree's spine prickled. The image of the railroad trestle over Trout Creek gorge jumped into her mind. The trains didn't use it much any more since the mines were closed, but kids walked across it when they were dared. And once every few months the police had to pull a body off the rocks below it. Drunks. Suicides.

Ree was on her bike again, pedaling back down street to 27, and Lisa followed. "What are you worried about?" Lisa yelled. "That he might get ugly drunk or something?"

"I just want to talk to him," Ree said, so softly Lisa didn't hear her.

The railroad crossed near the Amoco, then ran behind the single street of houses. Finally, at the edge of the woods, it crossed the curve of the river gorge and ran on the far side, opposite the ridge and opposite the old mine road. The spur that had once run to the mine was gone.

From the crest of 27 hill Rhiannon could see the trestle. No one on it but some kids. Nothing lying on the rocks.

She could not admit to Lisa what she was afraid of. She could hardly admit it even to herself. So she let her bike glide on down the hill, as if she had been going somewhere else all the time, and at the bottom stood the yellow metal gate. She sent her bike around it and into the woods on the old mine road.

"You think he's down here?" Lisa asked.

"Not really," Ree mumbled.

Lisa rolled her blue eyes and pedaled on in silence. The girls rode hard, quick and quiet, swooping down the narrow road with a swish of tires on gravel. They rounded the curve by the boulder pile—

With a snort the white Arabian raised his head from his grazing by the roadside, whirled and sprang away as lightly as a deer, leaping up the embankment, neck arched and tail streaming. He floated up the steep hillside as if it were air, the trees and thickets and rocks and fallen logs no more than cloud shadow, as if he had wings. Rhiannon had noted, numbly, that he definitely wore no halter, but Lisa gasped and swerved her bike to a stop. Eyes wide and mouth agape, she gawked after Angel.

"Ho-ly!" she gasped.

"Come on," Rhiannon said.

"Oh, wow, is he beautiful!" Still staring, Lisa had not moved.

"Never mind the horse for right now," Rhiannon urged impatiently. "We're looking for my father!" Though she had no reason to think he was anywhere near.

With a final toss of his elegant head, Angel galloped out of sight. But a noise came from another direction. Turning their heads, the girls could see something moving between the trees. A man. Ree stopped her bike.

"Speak of the devil," said Lisa. It was Bob DiAngelo.

Now that she finally saw him, Rhiannon found that she could not move or speak. She sat frozen on her bike, feet digging into the gravel, as he walked up to her. No beer smell on him, or maybe she just did not notice it out here in the fresh air of the woods. But he seemed sober. Cold sober, in the worst way. His stare was hard and cold.

"I'm sorry," she blurted out. "I mean, I never meant to, you know, hurt your feelings. I thought you were Shawn."

That sounded bad as she said it. Nothing seemed right. Her father's face hadn't changed. Why in the world had he come home when she was not expecting him? He never came home till suppertime. Sometimes not then.

"I've been looking all over for you," Ree added, trying hard to find the right words. Nothing she said seemed to affect him.

He finally spoke. "Well, don't," he said flatly.

What did he mean? "I know I'm grounded," Ree said, "but I had to talk with you."

"Don't bother." He glared her up and down as if she was some strange beast, then bared his teeth. "Grounded, ha." The laugh was a bark. "Go where you like. I don't care, right? Go ahead, ride horses, ride whatever. Stay out as late as you like. End up just like your Aunt Linda for all I care."

Aunt Linda? What did he mean? Aunt Linda was nice enough. She never had any money and she always looked tired, but almost all the grownups Rhiannon knew were like that. Sure, Aunt Linda had dropped out of high school to get married the first time, but so what? Everybody got married young in Hoadley. What else was there to do? You fell in love, you got married, you had babies. There was a joke about it. The first baby comes anytime, and after that they take nine months. Aunt Linda's first baby had only taken five months, and her first of several husbands had left her right after, but that wasn't her fault.

"You want to ruin your life, that's fine with me," Rhiannon's father told her, his teeth still showing in a grimace like a snarl. "Go ahead, do whatever you want. Just don't come running to me. Don't ask me for nothing."

"Dad—"

Teeth disappeared. He gave her a look more like hatred than anger. "Just let me alone!"

She sat staring at him and trying to think what to say. If she could just say the right thing, maybe—

"Get out of here!" His hands were balled into fists.

She turned her bike and went, pedaling hard, with Lisa by her side. Neither of them spoke all the way back to Rhiannon's house. Lisa hadn't said a word in front of Mr. DiAngelo.

"So much for talking with your father," she said finally, lamely, when they had dumped their bikes in Rhiannon's backyard.

Rhiannon felt numb. She had done so much angry crying during the night before that she had no energy left for any more emotion. "Thanks, Lisa," she said to her knees, sitting down on the stoop. "Thanks for coming with me."

"Well, at least you're not grounded anymore, huh?" Lisa sat beside her. "Going up to the horse place today?"

"I don't know." Rhiannon got up and went inside.

Even though it was past lunchtime, she did not feel hungry. She spent the afternoon doing load after load of laundry, washing dishes, cleaning the bathroom and her own room, working furiously every minute. By the time evening came she was too tired to go anywhere. She had even made supper, manicotti stuffed with imitation cheese and baked in tomato sauce, and she was on edge while it cooked, waiting for her father. But Bob DiAngelo did not come home for supper, and Ree's mother was at work, of course. Shawn and Deirdre ate with her.

Shawn devoured his manicotti with a ten-year-old's innocence, thinking nothing of it. Mothers and older sisters were meant to make good food for him. As for Deirdre, she seemed to scarcely know what she was eating, much less notice anything odd about her sister. She stared at an airy point somewhere above and behind Rhiannon's head, and there was a dreamy look in her eyes.

Beautiful, dark-haired Deirdre. She seemed as distant as a princess to Ree, sitting there in her frosted eye shadow and her mane of permed curl. Rhiannon had what her aunts and grandmothers called "big bones," which meant that she was husky and clumsy. Built like a horse, she had heard her cousins whisper with a snicker behind her back. She knew she would never be even half as pretty as Deirdre, and, what was worse, it was no use trying to talk to her. Years ago they had been friends, but when Deirdre had turned eleven or so she had started to detest her younger sister, and they had not really talked in a long time.

"Well," said Dee suddenly, "I have to get ready for my date with Keith." She left the table, aglow with beauty, and floated up the stairs, leaving the dishes for her sister. Of course.

" 'Bye," said Shawn, darting out.

Which lifeguard was Keith? Ree couldn't remember. She cleared the table and washed the dishes right then, even tired as she was, instead of leaving them for the next day. She meant for her father to find her scrubbing away in the kitchen. But when she finally heard him coming up the stoop she lost her nerve and ran upstairs to her room. Once there, she went to bed early, so exhausted that she slept without a dream. She had not even called Chickie to tell him she had seen his missing horse.

The next day she spent at Lisa's and her Grandma Phillips's, staying out of her father's way. And in the evening she went up the ridge to Chickie Miller's. He had work to do and couldn't go riding with her, but he showed her how to catch and saddle Hoss, and he let her ride up and down the farm lane. When she went up for her lesson on Sunday afternoon, she brought Hoss in and saddled him herself.

 **FIVE**

Rhiannon went to the Fourth of July Fireman's Carnival with Lisa and watched the plodding ponies with a superior smile. It no longer mattered that the new rules wouldn't let her lead them. Now she had a whole farm full of real horses to pat, groom, and ride. For almost three weeks she had been a regular evening visitor at Chickie Miller's place, and the Millers always welcomed her. They knew how to spell her name, where she lived, and when her birthday was. She had permission to saddle up Hoss and ride whenever she wanted. Already she felt secure at walk and trot, and she had even cantered Hoss up the lane a couple of times. Chickie had her riding him with a snaffle bit now instead of the bosal, and he was talking about having her exercise the other horses once she got more experienced. He was even talking about letting her ride down in the woods alone to look for the white Arabian.

"I think you're pulling the bull on me," he would tease. "You never seed him. You just want to ride my horses." Chickie himself had not seen Angel since the day the horse broke loose from him, though he and Ree had ridden down the ridge half a dozen times. There was a lot of wild country beyond the old mine for Angel to disappear into.

The woods felt like another world to Ree, and so did Chickie's farm, hidden down in the hollow, a sunny-side-of-the-ridge place where Mrs. Miller baked brownies, piled on white icing, and served them up to anyone who was handy. There were never any brownies or cookies at home anymore. Home was the place where Rhiannon's mother was tired and her father was best let alone. It had taken Ree several days to notice that Bob DiAngelo had stopped drinking, because he seemed more sullen than ever. But he stayed home instead of going to the Tipple, and he didn't even keep beer in the refrigerator. The more her father stayed home, though, the more Ree stayed away.

"Look at those poor things!" she said to Lisa, watching the ponies circle their ring, led by a machine with four metal arms. "Their hooves are worn all crooked and short in the toe. They need shoes."

Lisa sighed impatiently. "Like, jellies?"

"You goof, you know what I mean! They ought to be shod."

"Shot! Omigod, did they talk back or what?" Giggling, Lisa dove away as Rhiannon lunged at her. Ree chased her friend through the crowd, reaching for the plastic butterfly clips that held Lisa's red-blond hair in place. It would have been nice to have mussed that beautiful hair. But instead, Rhiannon bumped into Bucky Miller. Not too hard, though, and he was big enough to take it.

"Ooof! Sorry! Oh, hi, Bucky."

She had met him two or three times up at Chickie's, him and his brother, Hank. Bucky was the younger of the two boys, but he seemed old to her. He had to shave his beard every day, he had a driver's license, and he was almost out of high school. The older boy, Hank, was almost twenty but still lived at home. They both fooled with cars a lot, and they were both, Ree had to admit, really cute. They looked like the blond guy on "The Dukes of Hazzard."

"Hi, Bucky!" It was Lisa, with a lot more enthusiasm than Rhiannon had shown.

"Jeez, run a person over!" Soberly Bucky checked himself for injuries, making the girls giggle. A head taller than either of them, he was mostly muscle and mischief. "I guess I'm all right," he admitted at last, with such a doubtful look that both of them laughed aloud. "Buy you two airheads a Coke?"

His offer was welcome, as they had very little

spending money. Lisa was thrilled, though, for other reasons.

"Check it out!" Lisa whispered to Ree after they had giggled and chattered and drunk their sodas, when Bucky was sauntering away. She nudged her friend, eyes on Bucky's back, his shoulders showing off under a muscle shirt. "Hey, Ree, can I come horseback riding with you sometime?"

"I'll have to ask," Ree said seriously. "But you can't just get on the horse and ride. There's lots of things you have to learn. You want to have a tight, balanced seat, with your weight in your heels, and—"

"Oh, the heck with the horses," Lisa interrupted, still staring after Bucky. "I'll just come along up to the house."

"Aw, Lisa . . ." Ree felt disappointment crawl through her, then sighed in acceptance. "Don't wet your pants. Bucky's hardly ever there."

But he was there the next evening when she pedaled up to ride. He and Hank both. Rhiannon usually went to the Millers' in the evening because it was not so hot then, and also because Chickie would be there to coach her and help her. But this evening she did not see Chickie's truck by the house. It was a muggy day, and the bike ride had worn her out. She was dripping sweat.

"Chickie's not home yet," Mrs. Miller called from the shade of the porch. "Come sit here awhile and have some lemonade."

She did, grateful for the lemonade and the whoosh of an electric fan. Hank and Bucky were there too, sitting on an old metal glider, their long legs up and their booted feet on the railing.

"Don't know why he's so late," Mrs. Miller said. "He must've run into difficulties."

"How many did he have to shoe today?" Ree asked, sipping her lemonade.

"Not many. Just five, I think. Different places over near Hollis Corners."

Bucky called over from the other side of his mother, "Dad's one of the best farriers in the state, did you know that? People call him from clear down in York County. He goes down there to shoe the big standardbred farms. Most people around here don't know that. We sorta keep to ourselves."

"Bucky," said his mother, "it isn't good to brag." Her name was Bert, Rhiannon knew, though she had not yet realized it was short for Bertha. The name Bert suited her. When she closed her mouth hard and jutted her jaw, she looked very much the way a Bert should.

"Cripes," the older boy, Hank, drawled without looking around. "First you get down on us because we don't want to break our backs being like him. Then you get down on us because we say he's good."

Bert Miller sniffed and turned to Rhiannon, ignoring the boys. "Henry has always loved horses more than anything, all his life," she said. "It's too bad he married a woman who just likes them halfway, and raised children who don't care for them at all. He would have taught these boys to be farriers, but they didn't want that."

Puzzled, Ree asked, "Henry?"

"That's his real name. His nickname was Hen, and then people started calling him Chickie."

"Oh."

"Anyway, it's good for him, having you around. Gives him somebody to share his horses with."

"You just wait," Hank put in, "till he wants you to help him shoe."

Mrs. Miller turned to snap at him, but the rattling sound of Chickie's truck coming down the lane pulled her head around. First she looked, then she stared, then she rose to her feet with a tense look on her face.

"Oh, Lordy. What now?"

Towed behind the pickup's sideboards and forge, a horse trailer came wobbling down the lane.

Chickie pulled up by one of the sheds, and all of them, even Hank and Bucky, walked out to meet him. But Ree stiffened when he got out of the cab. She had not realized how much she counted on Chickie's sawtoothed smile, and it was gone. She had never seen him look so angry and grim.

"Everybody stay back," he ordered, and he went to the trailer, slid out the ramp and opened the doors. Rhiannon could hear him talking softly as he disappeared inside. Like the others she edged back, expecting a wild-eyed stallion to come rampaging out.

Instead, she saw a filthy, tangled tail draggling down from under a green horse blanket. Then a blanketed rump—the horse backed down the ramp very slowly, staggering with every step. Something, she didn't know what, was wrong with it. There were swarms of flies buzzing around it, and something smelled bad. What was wrong? The horse teetered on its hooves, acting as if it could scarcely walk. But when she saw the stark bones of the neck and shoulders, the skeletal look of the head, she had to put her hand to her mouth to keep from screaming or crying.

"My God, Henry," said Mrs. Miller sharply, "the thing's all over lice!"

There was hardly any hair on the parts of the horse Rhiannon could see, and what little there was grew long and wispy, as if vainly trying to cover the black skin.

"I know it, Bert, and you don't have to let me in the house, I'll sleep in the shed with him. I'll have to nurse him tonight, anyways. Now, you're not going to tell me I should have left this creature there to die."

"No," she said firmly. "No, I'm not. But I am going to tell you we have to get rid of some of the others. You can't just keep on—"

Chickie turned his back to lead the stumbling horse into the shed. "Got to get him in a stall," he boomed, "before he falls down. Had to rig a sling in the trailer."

"You can't just keep on bringing home the hard

luck horses," Bert shouted after him, "and never sell any once they're better. We'll go in the poorhouse!"

"What's one more?" Chickie shouted back. "I raise the hay and oats, I shoe 'em myself, I worm 'em—would somebody get some straw?"

Rhiannon jerked out of her staring stupor to hurry into the barn, but Bucky was there before her. He threw bales of straw down from the loft, then climbed down and helped her carry them to the shed and spread a thick bed in the stall where sick horses were put, separate from the barn and the other horses. The instant they were done, Chickie led the new horse in, and he barely got the blanket off before the ghastly-looking animal collapsed. Mrs. Miller came to stand beside Chickie, but not too close for fear of lice. She stood looking down into the stall with a hard set to her mouth.

"The house is paid for, woman!" he grumbled, though she had not said anything.

"A person would like a nice dress once in a while, instead of all the time vet bills," Bert stated. "That's all I'm saying, and then I won't say no more."

"Good!" Chickie snapped.

"It's a blessing that blasted Arab run off, if you ask me," Bert added, though no one had asked her and she was not supposed to say anymore. "One less to vet. There, I'm done."

Chickie looked at her, rolled his eyes, and piled hay into the stall with sharp movements of his hands. The horse did not get up, but snaked out its

67

terribly thin neck and began to nibble at the food. Wadded bits of hay dribbled out of the corners of its mouth.

"God!" Chickie exploded. "The poor thing can't even chew. Hope he lives till Doc Shaffer gets here. How can people be so—so—" He gave up, shaking his head.

"Where did you find it?" Mrs. Miller asked in a resigned tone. Rhiannon still could not speak. She was almost too horrified to move. Staring, she saw every rib of the starved horse's sides, saw how its hipbones jutted like a cow's, saw the gaunt hollows where there should have been muscle.

"You remember that woman called a few days back? Said Donna MacAdams give her our name? Said something was wrong with her horse's feet? Well, I had to go shoe Donna's barn today, so I stopped by. And something's wrong, okay." The words shivered with Chickie's anger. Rhiannon had never heard him so harshly angry. "Gelding's got thrush in all four feet from standing in shit for months on end."

"Henry!" Mrs. Miller reproved. "Think of the girl."

Rhiannon found her voice. "That's okay," she muttered, feeling sick, but not from Chickie's language. He looked at her and saw it.

"Ree, you don't want to hear this, you can go."

She managed to meet his eyes. "I want to know what happened."

"Okay. Though I don't understand it myself, how some people can be such jerks. Ignorant. Worse than ignorant, just plain—"

"Henry," Bert warned. He took a deep breath and went on.

"They had a corner of the garage turned into a stall. A concrete slab for the horse to stand on or lie on. No pasture, not even a turnout. Horse stood in its stall, day in, day out. See the sores on his hips and elbows, where they dug through the crap and came up against the concrete when he lay down?"

On the horse's belly, also, Rhiannon saw, there were patches of raw pink skin with red, oozing centers. She steadied herself against the stall boards with one hand.

"The jackass of a husband had the nerve to tell me somebody told them not to feed the horse too much, since it wasn't getting much exercise." Chickie bit his words into hard pebbles to hurl. "Don't look to me like he was fed too much. What you think?"

"So what did you do?" Bucky spoke for the first time.

"I just stood there with my teeth hanging out. I was shook, like Ree here, I couldn't say nothing." Chickie gave Rhiannon a kindly look. He was beginning to get his smile back. "And there was this . . . this . . . birdbrain of a woman standing at my elbow prattling about how the horse's condition was down because he was just recovering from an infection. I bet. Doubt he's been vetted in years. Probably full of worms as well as lice. Anyways, I just up and left. Said something about needing a special tool, and I took off. Went down the road to Donna's. Told her what I just seen—she was shocked, had no idea. Barely knew the people. Thought they boarded their horse someplace. So I borrowed the blanket and the trailer and went back. Told the darling couple they had a choice. They could hand over the horse to me right then, or I could go to the Humane Society and come back with a cop and a warrant. Didn't take them long to make up their minds. I think they wanted the horse off their hands, or they wouldn't of let nobody see it. Probably didn't know what they was going to do with the body. They just went inside the house. I loaded the horse and left."

Rhiannon filled a plastic bucket with water from the barn hose, then lugged it to the new horse's stall. She wanted to do something for him. But Chickie stopped her with a gesture before she could put it inside.

"Just set it down, I'll put it in when he wants it. Don't want you going in there, you might catch lice."

"Shouldn't we . . . give him a bath, or something?" she asked timidly.

"Can't do nothing with him right now. He's so weak and worn out from the trip, I don't want to make him stand up. Hank. Where's Hank?"

Hank lounged forward. He seemed always to be half asleep.

Chickie said, "Do me a favor. Go down the drugstore and get me some film for the Polaroid and some of them flash bars. I want to take pictures of this hard luck horse. Case those idiots change their minds, I want something to show the judge."

Hank nodded and slouched out. In a moment Rhiannon heard the roar of his California-raked GTO heading up the lane. Chickie said, "Bert."

She just looked at him, her jaw jutting like that of a snapping turtle.

"We still got any of that louse shampoo for people and animals both?"

Curtly she told him, "Yes. Plenty."

"First thing in the morning I'll get this gelding up and dress his hooves. Then I got to shower and get to work. So leave me the shampoo and some clothes in the basement. And I want you to get the horse cleaned up before Doc Shaffer comes."

"Does it occur to you," said Mrs. Miller frostily, "that I got other things to do? I got errands to run over Canadawa." Bert's people were from the other side of the mountain, and she still went there to see her mother and shop.

"You got to be here for the vet," said Chickie. "If I got to miss a day of work, it won't help your new-dress fund none." He didn't sound angry anymore, just tired.

"That ain't the point. You bring home a lousy horse, you ought to be the one who—"

71

Rhiannon said, "I'll bathe him." Bert and Chickie both stopped in midquarrel and looked at her, but Ree made sure she didn't look at Bert.

"You sure you can?" said Chickie slowly. "You ever bath a horse before?"

Bucky, who had been standing silently by, said in a doomed tone, "I'll help her. I got the morning off."

"Heck fire, boy, why didn't you say so before?"

"Because I knew what would happen," Bucky said. "Spend it washing a miserable stinking horse. Way to go." He sighed and ambled back toward the house. His mother followed. Rhiannon wanted to go, too, but her own horror kept her standing where she was, looking at the starved horse.

Lying in the straw and lipping his hay, with almost all his flesh gone, the gelding looked like a goblin horse, big headed, helpless as a newborn foal, with long, sticklike legs and shrunken flanks. The light in the stall was dim enough so that Ree could not see the crawling lice, but she saw the belly bloated with worms and the sore places where the hard floor had rubbed. There was so little hair left on the horse that she could not tell what color he was. She felt awash in strangeness—a horse was not supposed to look like this. Horses were proud and strong. Trying to make a connection with this horse, Ree asked, "What's his name?"

Chickie looked over at her with a shadow of his elfin grin. "You know, I didn't ask."

They both stood silently looking at the gelding for

a minute. Then with a sudden surge of anger Ree said, "We wouldn't want to call him what they called him, anyway."

"You said it, sis. What you want to name him?"

Rhiannon said, "I—I don't know. It's hard to tell what he's really like."

"Wait and see if he lives," drawled a different voice. Hank was at the shed door, bringing the camera and film.

"No!" Ree exclaimed, too loudly. Her stomach hurt. "We'll name him right now."

Chickie looked at her and nodded. "Sure, he deserves to have a name. Whatever you say is fine with me."

Rhiannon stood with her mouth open, waiting for the name to come out.

Chickie said, "If that Arab son of a gun is Angel, maybe this poor cuss is Devil or something."

Ree shook her head. There was a name, her favorite horse name for years and years, and she had always wanted to give it to a horse of her own. But suddenly she decided that this starved, sick horse could have it.

"Let's call him Prince," she said.

Hank set down the camera on the stall ledge and went away, snorting and snickering. Chickie didn't blink an eye. "That's okay with me," he said.

It was time for Ree to go home. "Good night, Prince," she said to the horse, and he looked at her, turning his ears toward the sound of her voice. She headed out the door, then stopped and looked back at the bowlegged farrier leaning against the stall. He would sit down on a bale of hay after a while. He would be with the horse all night.

"Bring you a sandwich or something?" Ree offered.

"Thanks. But you know, I ain't hungry. Things like this, they really take it out of me, anymore. Anyhow, I don't need it." Chickie grinned and slapped the bulge of his belly.

Crossing the barnyard, though, Rhiannon passed Mrs. Miller. Bert was heading toward the shed with a coffeepot and a plate of cold chicken, pickles, onion rolls, and potato salad.

SIX

The next morning Rhiannon's bike had a flat tire.

"Crud!" she muttered, standing in the garage. It was a few minutes past 6 A.M., and there she stood in her oldest jeans, ready to go nurse the horse that had troubled her sleep all night. And no bike. She could start walking, but it would take her close to an hour to get up the ridge. She might even miss the vet.

Bracing herself, she headed back inside. Her father was watching "Morning Stretch" on TV. Then he would watch the local news and the "Today Show." He always got up early, a habit left over from his working days. But he had no place to go.

"Dad," Rhiannon requested, "would you patch my bike tire for me, please?"

He looked at her as if she had two heads.

"I'm supposed to be someplace," Ree said.

75

"I told you, don't ask me for nothing." Bob DiAngelo turned his eyes back to the athletic woman on TV.

Rhiannon had no time to argue with him or be angry at him. She headed out, thinking. If she hunted and found the patch kit, she might be able to fix the tire herself. It was a new thought—her father had always done it for her before. But it would take too long to find the kit and learn how. Maybe Hank at the Amoco would do it. But she was half afraid of him and all the other rough men in there, turning the air thick with cursing. She'd sooner walk up the ridge— Wait. Lisa's bike.

She went down the alley and got it out of the Toth garage. Nobody in 27 bothered to lock a house, let alone a garage. What was worth stealing? Rhiannon doubted if Lisa would be wanting her bike even when she finally got up, close to noon, and Rhiannon might be back by then.

She pedaled hard all the way to the Miller place and went straight to the shed. Puffing, sweating, and dreading what she might see, she looked into the stall. . . . Prince was on his feet, tearing at his hay.

"You're up!" Ree said gladly.

He staggered toward the sound of her voice and thrust his bony head at her. Even as horrible as he looked, she longed to touch him.

"Oh, poor baby, I wish I could pat you. But we have to get rid of the lice first, or I'll be in trouble."

Bucky walked in. "Phew," he said, wrinkling his

nose as he came near the stall. The stench from the new horse was no better than it had been the night before. "Yecch! Barf," Bucky said.

"At least he's up!" Ree snapped.

"Dad got him up and dressed his feet about an hour ago. Took a shower in the basement, deloused himself and went to work. Mom's boiling the horse blanket and grouching. Let's get this wonder horse out where we can breathe."

"His name's Prince," Rhiannon told Bucky.

"I know. Dad said." Bucky slid open the stall door and snapped a lead rope onto the gelding's halter. "Come on, boy," he coaxed. "Come on, wonder horse. It's a wonder you're not dog food. Come on, get moving."

"Take it easy with him!" Ree exclaimed as the horse plunged forward, and Bucky rolled his eyes.

He did, he took it very easy in spite of all his mocking talk. Rhiannon should have known no son of Chickie's would be mean to a horse. And Prince was pitifully willing, moving at once toward the sound of a human voice, desperate to please. Hobbling along on bandaged hooves that were half trimmed away because of the thrush, the infection in his feet. So brave. After ten minutes Bucky had the horse standing in the barnyard, and Rhiannon didn't care about lice anymore. She patted and patted Prince on the neck. Bucky's mother came down from the house, where she had been standing on the porch, watching. "The poor thing's suffering," she said. "He should be put out of his misery, and so should some of the others."

Rhiannon looked up at her, feeling a chill. Bucky yawned.

"You want me to have you put out of your misery when you start suffering, Ma?" he asked, straight-faced.

Bert's chin started to jerk. Ignoring her son, she turned to Ree. "I guess you think I'm a regular old witch," she said.

Rhiannon did, sort of, but she didn't want Mrs. Miller to be mad at her. And anybody who made brownies like Mrs. Miller's couldn't be too much of a witch. Ree shook her head.

"I can see you do. But you'll understand me better when you're grown. Henry's a good man, and I wouldn't want him any different than just the way he is. And he works harder than any two people I know. But it all goes to feed horses."

On the other side of the horse, Bucky rolled his eyes skyward. I've heard all this before, his look said. "Ma," he begged, "get the lousy shampoo, would you?"

"You got to clip him first. The lice hide in the hair." Wearily Mrs. Miller went to find horse clippers and an orange extension cord.

She stood and watched the clipping. Bucky held the horse in case the electric clippers spooked it, but Prince was either calm about the buzzing noise or too weak to fuss. Rhiannon clipped, starting at the head, shearing away sparse patches of hair and what little was left of the mane.

"Go easy around the sores," Bert told her when she got to the belly, though Ree was already clipping so carefully and gently that Bucky was jiggling his knees with impatience.

"Can I leave the tail?" Ree asked. "He'll need something to swish flies with." She hated to think of a horse with a shaved tail. Bert considered.

"Clip the root, I guess, and just leave a swish on the tip. We'll have to make sure we wash it good. Bucky, don't you think you'd better wait till the day warms up some before you bath him? You'll give the poor thing a chill."

"Time we get some buckets of warm water out here," Bucky said, "it'll be hot enough."

Mrs. Miller raised her eyebrows. Buckets of warm water were a lot of extra work. Horses were usually hosed down to be washed, just like cars, with the cold water that came out of the outdoor spigot. But Bert only blinked once, then turned and went. By the time Ree and Bucky were done clipping, she had brought three buckets full of strong-smelling delousing suds. Then Rhiannon took her turn holding the lead rope, and Bucky went to work.

He sopped his sponge quickly but gently, working his way from the head back, making sure he wiped every inch of the horse for lice. Then he did it again. Prince stood quietly. Whenever Rhiannon spoke to him, he turned toward her to nuzzle her.

"Careful around the eyes," Mrs. Miller told her son.

"Ma, I thought you said you had things to do."

She gave him a grumpy look but did not go away except to replace the buckets of dirty suds with clear warm water for rinsing.

"Ma!" Bucky demanded. "You got some sort of big, old towel or blanket? To wrap him, like."

"You don't want to rub him," Bert said, "with his skin the way it is. Poor thing."

"Just something to throw over him."

She went into the house and came out a few minutes later with an old chenille bedspread. Bert held one side and Ree the other, and they lifted it high over the horse before letting it down gently on him. Prince was so tottery that Ree felt as if the weight of it might knock him down. But he stood stolidly. The spread covered him from poll to tail and dragged in the mud on either side. Bert gathered it together in front of his chest and fastened it with a huge safety pin left over from her cloth-diaper days.

"There," she said.

Prince laid his nose against her neck. Since he was deloused, Mrs. Miller did not object, though she had not touched him before. She patted him briefly.

"Such a kind eye he has," she remarked, "after all he's been through." She backed away. "I got to go see my ma and run my errands. Don't neither of you go inside, not for nothing. Just the thought of what might be on you makes me itch." She shuddered, scratched herself, then headed into the house. A minute later her car crunched its dusty way up the lane.

Bucky remarked, "Ma's scared she might have to like that horse."

Head down and eyes blinking, Prince stood dozing in the sun under his bedspread. Bucky let the lead rope drop, went over to the barn door and sat on the sill. "He ain't going nowhere," he said. "Hurts him too much to walk."

Ree sat on the other end of the sill from Bucky to wait for the vet.

It took a while. Prince baked dry and Ree and Bucky took the bedspread off him, and still no Doc Shaffer. The two kids were talking about whether to move the horse back into the stall, where his hay was, or bring some hay and water out to him, when the rattle of gravel finally announced a vehicle. Ree grabbed Prince's lead rope, and the vet's customized Bronco nosed its way out from between the overgrown apple trees.

Ree held the lead rope short, with both hands, but Prince was too weak or docile to spook, even when the vet pulled up close by him. Doc Shaffer got out from behind the wheel.

"Good Lord," he said, staring.

He was a slim, stooped man with quick hands, quick speech, and a quick step—but the sight of the hard luck horse stopped him in his tracks for a moment. "Good Lord," he repeated. "Where did Chickie find it?"

Without waiting for an answer to his own question, he brought out his instruments, looked into the gelding's eyes and mouth, listened to heart and lungs, felt the legs. "Dad wants him tube wormed," Bucky said.

"Too weak." Doc still looked shocked. "Weight's a good two hundred pounds down. No flesh at all, no muscle tone, no resistance. Suppurating abcesses in his hooves, infected sores on his belly, elbows, hips, sheath. If deworming makes him a little sick, it might take him right off."

Ree felt cold, listening. Prince was close to death.

"What do we do, then?" Bucky asked.

"I'll just give him paste dewormer, maybe a quarter dose, and some antibiotics so we can start to get the infection under control. We have to try to build him up slowly. I can float his teeth." Doc went to his truck.

"What does he mean, float his teeth?" Ree whispered to Bucky.

"File down the long edges, so he can chew better."

Doc Shaffer came back with a rasp, grasped Prince by the nose and filed away at his teeth with a grating sound. He worked for quite a while, and Prince stood still as a stump. "Worst mouth I've ever seen," the vet muttered. Finally he straightened up and stepped back. "There. Now maybe he'll get more good out of his food."

"Dad's afraid to give him grain," Bucky said.

"Maybe just a handful, but then watch him for colic. Your dad's right, it might be too much for him. Even good timothy hay might be too much for him. But you have to take a little risk. You can't keep starving him."

The vet swabbed the gelding's neck with alcohol and gave him an injection. With a syringe he squirted the worming paste into Prince's mouth. He searched in his Bronco, then handed Bucky a large tube of ointment for the sores. Bucky passed it to Rhiannon.

"Do you have him bedded on straw?" Doc Shaffer asked Bucky. "Sawdust will stick to those sores."

"We got straw. Dad always keeps some around for sick horses."

"How's his manure?"

"Almost as stinky as his hooves," said Bucky.

He and the vet went to get a sample out of the stall, to be analyzed for worms. Ree put ointment on all the sores she could reach without letting go of the lead rope. Then she stood stroking the gelding, hearing Doc Shaffer seriously speaking as he came out of the shed.

"I'll be back in three days, and I really think if he hasn't gotten stronger by then, your father ought to consider having him put down."

Rhiannon's hand stopped its stroking. Prince nudged her in the ribs. Then, as the vet walked briskly past on his way to his truck, the lanky gelding stretched out his head and neck toward him. Doc Shaffer stopped.

"Well," he said in surprise, "after all that, you're friendly, boy? Maybe you'll make it after all." He rubbed the horse gently on the cheekbones, then got into his truck and drove off. Both Rhiannon's hands curled tightly around the lead rope as she watched him go.

"They can't kill Prince," she said fiercely. "They just can't. He's too . . . too . . ."

"Just don't say anything to Mom about that part," Bucky told her. "Watch him a few minutes, would you? I got to shovel out that stall and spray for lice."

Rhiannon stroked the horse while Bucky worked. She would gladly have stood and patted him for hours, but she knew Prince had to rest. After Bucky was done with the stall, Ree helped him get Prince back into it. She put ointment on all the sores, made sure Prince had plenty of hay and water, then left him.

Mrs. Miller was back from Canadawa and taking charge. She made first Bucky, then Rhiannon, shower in the basement cinder-block shower and shampoo with the louse shampoo Chickie had used in the morning. She gave Ree some outgrown clothes of Bucky's to wear and put the others in boiling water. Even Ree's jogging shoes were doused with boiling water and detergent. Finally, squeaky clean and barefoot, Ree was allowed upstairs for lunch.

Ree felt better about Mrs. Miller after she had

finished her bacon and tuna sandwich, a plate of spaghetti, and two cupcakes. Bucky had already eaten and gone to work.

After lunch Ree went out to check on the horse again. Prince was down in the clean straw, flat on his side with his neck stretched out, and for a horrible moment she thought he was dead. There were flies on him. Then she saw the movement of his bony ribs. He was sleeping.

He must be too weak to shake the flies off, Ree decided. They were clustering around his eyes and on his sores. Softly she went into the stall with him and chased them off. She made herself a fan of hay and sat in the straw beside the horse, keeping the flies away.

It was a hot, drowsy afternoon, full of summerbug hum. Ree swished flies for a long time. She nodded and yawned, and her arm seemed to move by itself. Somewhere a phone rang, buzzing like the summerbugs. She paid no attention.

"Ree - ANN - on!" It was Bert Miller, hollering from the porch. "Phone!"

She blinked, stumbled up and went over to take the call at the barn extension. It was Chickie. "How's the Prince?" he wanted to know.

"The vet—Doc said—" Ree hesitated, wondering if Mrs. Miller might be listening on the house phone, then decided to chance it. "He says he's real weak. If he's not better when he comes back in three days, he wants to put him down."

"Doc's an old wet blanket," Chickie boomed into the phone. "Always has been. Prepares you for the worst. What's that horse doing right now?"

"Lying down in the straw, sleeping. He's breathing, but he hasn't moved in hours."

"He can sleep tonight," Chickie said. "Wake him up and make him eat. Are we supposed to grain him?"

"A little."

"Give him a handful of oats, then, and watch him. If he starts thrashing around or biting or kicking at his stomach, get him on his feet and call me right away. Bert knows where I am." Chickie hung up.

With chirping sounds and gentle swats Ree awakened the horse and offered him hay, letting him lie where he was and eat it. When he seemed a little more alert she gave him the oats, then sat watching, worried by every movement. When Prince heaved himself to his feet to drink water, she put ointment on his sores again, and the horse swung his wet muzzle around and nuzzled her. All through the afternoon and past suppertime she stayed with him, until Chickie came home and took over.

How could they think of killing him? Prince was too sweet and brave to die.

Taking off her still-wet running shoes inside the back door, dead tired, Ree glanced up to find her father standing over her. She was startled, for she was not yet used to finding her father in the house.

But she was too bone-tired and heartsore to really jump.

"I fixed your tire," Bob DiAngelo said angrily.

Ree had been worried about her bike, and she reacted to what he said rather than his angry tone. "Thanks," she told him, meaning it.

"Where you been all day?"

"Nursing a sick horse." She wobbled into the kitchen as if she were sick herself, washed her hands, then started blindly hunting in the refrigerator.

"Siddown," her father ordered. "What do you mean, a sick horse? What's the matter with it?"

"Everything. These people, like, they neglected it, they didn't do what they were supposed to. I mean, they didn't feed it right or anything." Seated at the table, Ree lifted her hands, trying to explain, knowing she could not explain how the horse made her heart ache. "It's got worms, and, like, rot in its feet, and it's so skinny and starved it's almost ready to die, and it's got these awful sores—"

She blinked. Food had appeared before her, macaroni and cheese that her father had kept warm in the oven. He plopped a hot dog in front of her.

"I cooked, for once," Bob DiAngelo said belligerently. "Nothing else to do. Eat it."

She did, willingly. Her father sat across from her, watching with hard eyes.

"And I did the bleeping laundry," he barked. "Some of it."

87

Ree's attention was still on the macaroni and cheese. "You made this?" she marveled. "It's good."

"What the hun, it ain't hard. Just read the box. I don't know why women make such a fuss about cooking."

Ree ate hungrily, which seemed to satisfy him. He sat back and relaxed.

"How'd you get up to that place?" he asked after a while.

"Lisa's bike. Omigod." Ree wiped her mouth and started to get up. "I never called her."

"Siddown," Bob DiAngelo ordered. "Eat." He got up, went and made the phone call himself, then came back. "She never missed it."

"Thanks," Rhiannon said.

"Huh. You going to stay home and help me with the laundry tomorrow?"

To Ree's surprise her eyes filled with tears. "Dad, I have to go back up to take care of Prince."

"Huh," her father said, and he turned his back, went out to the other room, and sat in front of the TV.

SEVEN

The next few days Rhiannon was scarcely ever home at all. Dawn to dusk she was at the Miller place, and not riding, either. She had forgotten about riding; she had forgotten about Angel, the white Arabian; she had forgotten there were horses other than Prince in the world. From the time Chickie left for work in the morning until the time he came back at night, she was with the sick gelding. She cleaned his stall the moment he soiled it so that he would not get worse infection in his skin or his feet. She hand-fed him hay and tiny amounts of oats every hour throughout the day, making sure Prince ate even when he felt too tired to bother. She kept his sores covered with ointment. Sometimes she just talked to him, and Prince never failed to stretch his head out toward her to be patted on his scrawny, naked neck.

The borrowed horse blanket had been boiled to

kill lice, then dried, and Chickie was putting it on Prince at night to keep the horse warm, hairless as he was. Rhiannon had to judge whether or not to take it off during the days, whether Prince was too hot or too cold. Sometimes she gently led him outside to get some fresh air and doze in the sun, and then she had to judge how soon to take him back in. Prince might get overtired, or he might get sunburn. He was so weak, the least little thing could kill him.

Hard as she tried, Rhiannon could not see any difference in Prince by the time Doc Shaffer came back.

The vet did not see any either. "He's not responding," Doc Shaffer said darkly.

Chickie was there. It was a Saturday afternoon, late, and he usually came home a few hours earlier on Saturdays. "Lordy, man, look at the bright side," he boomed at Doc Shaffer. "The horse is holding his own."

"And suffering every minute. Maybe you ought to think about having him put down."

"Heck, no," said Chickie promptly, without even looking at Rhiannon. "He's got to start getting better soon. Rhiannon, here, she's just taking too good of a care of him, is all. Got him spoiled."

Doc Shaffer looked at Rhiannon, seemed about to say something, then decided against it. He gave Prince more worm medicine and more antibiotics, talked with Chickie for a while about the condition of the horse's feet, then rattled away in his Bronco, going home for supper.

Rhiannon had taken Prince into his stall and put the blanket on him. After the vet was gone Chickie came in there, selected a straw to chew, and looked at the horse.

"Doc says try just a little more grain," he told Rhiannon.

"Okay."

"Can you stay till I get some supper? Then I'll take over." Chickie had a beat-up old sleeping bag spread out on the bales of straw near Prince's stall. He had been spending his nights with the horse, and Bert had been making sour jokes about it.

"Sure," said Ree. "I'll wait around and help you dress his hooves."

"I'll let you baby-sit him while I do my chores, then." Chickie poured a half scoop of grain into the gelding's feed bucket, then left.

Prince, on his feet, ate the grain without having to be coaxed. He is getting better, Rhiannon thought boldly, only half believing it. Clean your plate, that's a good boy. I bet Chickie is cleaning his plate. Get better, Prince. Get strong.

She watched the gelding and hummed to herself. Mrs. Miller brought her ham potpie and a sticky bun. Rhiannon gulped the potpie and gave the empty plate back to Bert, who nodded and headed back to the house. Ree ate the bun, then sat licking syrup off her fingers. She felt contented and sleepy. It was dusk outside. Sparrows were chittering, Chickie was clattering around in the barn, feeding the other horses, and Prince was moving around in his stall. Maybe he really was getting better. Usually his feet hurt him so badly that he never moved unless he had to. . . .

Prince swung his head with a puzzled look and bit at his blanketed side.

Rhiannon sat straight up and stared at him. Prince staggered in an uneasy circle around his stall, lifted one hind foot and kicked at his own belly. Ree jumped up and turned on the single bare light bulb that hung overhead. She saw a flash of white in Prince's eyes, and there was a thin sheen of sweat on the gelding's neck.

She screamed as loud as she could, "Chickie!" The sound of her voice must have told him to come quick. She heard the thud as he dropped a plastic feeding bucket, and he came out of the barn door and toward her at his rolling, bearlike run. She opened Prince's stall door and stood patting him, not knowing what else to do. The horse was shaking all over, holding his head high and stiff, rolling his eyes in fear.

"Colic," said Chickie from the other side of the stall boards. "Get a good hold on that halter, Ree, and whatever you do, don't let him get down. Make him walk if you have to, keep him moving, but don't let him roll. I think I got a shot around here somewhere, but I better talk with Doc first." He sprinted toward the house.

Rhiannon stood with the horse, too scared to think of anything except: Don't let him roll. Prince was swinging his head up, down, from side to side. She held onto the chin strap of the halter, the way Chickie had showed her a week or two back. Up at the house she heard the screen door slam. Somebody came into the shed and stood on the opposite side of the stall boards, but it couldn't be Chickie back already—

"Don't you think you ought to come home for a change?"

Startled by the familiar voice in the place where it didn't belong, Rhiannon stared at her father blankly for an instant. Then she wailed, "Dad! Not now! Prince has colic!"

Bob DiAngelo's scowling gaze shifted to the horse, and shock or surprise lifted his black eyebrows out of their frown. "What the hun!" he exclaimed.

Prince buckled his knees and plunged toward his straw, nearly pulling his halter out of Rhiannon's grasp. "No!" she screamed, planting her feet and tugging strongly against him. She got him back up. "Dad, hand me that lead rope, quick! I've got to get him out of here and make him walk."

For not knowing what a lead rope was, Bob DiAngelo found it pretty fast. He handed it to Ree and watched as she clipped it on, shouldered the stall door open and half coaxed, half wrestled Prince out onto the dirt floor, then out the shed door into the barnyard. The pain in his belly made the horse fight against her. He wanted to get down and thrash and roll, but Ree managed to keep him up and moving. Chickie barreled down past her from the house, shouted something, and disappeared into the barn.

"Come on, Prince," Ree panted, coaxing, "come on, good boy. Poor baby. You have to stay on your feet!"

"What's going on?" her father asked from behind her. "Is that the horse you were telling me about?"

Ree nodded. "Colic," she yelled, as if that explained everything, as if everyone knew that colic could kill a horse. Prince was weaving wildly from side to side, tottering on his sore feet, nearly falling. Rhiannon skittered along at his shoulder, walking half backward, watching the horse and jumping from side to side to pull on his head, push at his neck or shoulder, whatever seemed likely to keep him upright. "Come on, Prince!" she begged him.

"Okay, Ree, just hold him still a minute till I get this shot in him." Out of the dusk Chickie appeared by her side, holding a hypodermic. "Doc'll be here soon as he can."

Holding Prince still was not easy. Rhiannon braced her back against his chest, held onto his halter with both hands and talked to him. Chickie held him by the nose and quickly, as if it were easy, gave him the shot in the neck.

"Good. Okay, I got him, Ree." Chickie took the lead rope from her, and limply she went over to stand beside her father. Bob DiAngelo had not moved from the doorway of the shed, but somebody else had joined him there. It was Bucky, his hands still black with grease from his Amoco job.

"Hi," Ree said to him tiredly.

"Dad sent me down in case you needed me," Bucky said. "Poor weak little girl that you are."

"Big help you were," Ree retorted.

"Shoot, it looked to me like you could muscle that gelding okay. I was starting to feel sorry for him."

The three of them stood for a while and watched as Chickie did what Rhiannon had been doing with Prince, keeping the horse moving to keep him on his feet.

"What's colic?" Rhiannon's father asked her.

"It's just, like, a bellyache. But if the horse gets down and rolls, it can twist his guts up and he can die."

"It's a blockage," Bucky said. "He'll be okay once his fuel line gets flowing again."

"Oh." Bob DiAngelo watched awhile longer. "Funny animals, horses," he said finally.

Bucky laughed. "That one's funnier than most."

Prince was starting to feel better as the pain reliever Chickie had given him took hold. He stopped fighting, his eyes calmed down, his ears listened when Chickie talked to him. Chickie stopped him and let him stand still for a while. The big man bent

95

over and put his ear to the horse's side, listening. Rhiannon ran over to Prince and patted him, talking softly to him. More slowly her father followed. He and Chickie spoke briefly, the way men do when they first meet, outwardly friendly but sizing each other up, shaking hands and judging each other by the handshake. Chickie seemed very tired. He wasn't saying much, not even to Rhiannon. "Don't keep your dad waiting," he told her. "You going to stay home tomorrow? See you Monday, I guess."

"Is Prince going to be okay?"

"Probably. Could be hours, though, before he's really over it."

Ree was scared. Chickie didn't usually say probably. He usually said, "Sure thing." Rhiannon said to her father, "Dad, I want to stay."

"No," he told her.

"If he passes some of them worms," Chickie said, "he'll be fine. Worms is what's doing it to him. You call me in the morning, Ree, I'll tell you how he is."

Rhiannon stroked Prince high on his neck, near his ears, and he nuzzled her, then stretched his long neck briefly and lipped at her father's shirt. With a huge sigh he turned back to Ree and rested his forehead against her chest.

"G'night, Prince," Rhiannon said, and she said good night to Chickie and Bucky and walked off with her father.

The lane was very dark. She could not see her father's face. She could barely see the car until they were right at it and Bob DiAngelo opened the driver's side door so that the dome light went on. Then Ree went around and got in on her side. "What about my bike?" she asked.

"Do you have time to walk up tomorrow and get it? Or I could put it in the trunk."

"I'll come and get it."

They were both very quiet and very polite, as if they felt afraid they might get into a fight about something if they weren't. Bob DiAngelo sat for a minute as if he thought Ree might say something else, then started the car and sent it up the lane in first gear.

"Why did you come to get me?" Ree asked.

"I thought I'd come visit with you for a change. Got nothing better to do."

"Oh, really." Ree's politeness slipped, but her father kept his.

"Yes, really. You don't believe me?"

Ree said bluntly, "No."

"Why not?"

"You could visit with me in the daytime. You came right at dark."

"Your mom had the car all day."

That was true. Rhiannon sat in silence for a minute, then said stubbornly, "I think you were checking on me."

"How come?"

"I just do. I know the way you think. You were checking on me."

Bob DiAngelo was silent for a minute, swinging the car past the Amoco station. "Okay," he said at last in a tough voice, "so I do care about you after all."

Rhiannon couldn't say a word. It was the nearest her father had ever come to saying he loved her. She wished she could reach over and kiss him.

"So you listen to me, sis. I've heard about those Miller boys. They're supposed to be pretty wild. Now, you—"

"Oh, *Dad!*" Ree wailed, her loving mood shattered. "I just go up there because of the horses!"

Bob DiAngelo pulled the car up the alley and into the cinder-block garage that squatted right by the pavement. Then he opened his car door a crack, so that the light came on overhead, and he leveled a long, narrow-eyed look at his daughter.

"I saw how that Bucky looked at you," he said.

Rhiannon felt her jaw drop. Bob DiAngelo saw her surprise, and his tone gentled.

"You really aren't thinking about boys yet? Okay, honey. I know you're only twelve, but you're built just about as big as Deirdre, and—"

The name jarred. *"I'm not Deirdre!"* Rhiannon shouted, suddenly furious, and she lunged out of the car and ran into the house before her father could answer.

Her mother was there, sitting slumped at the table with her hands sprawling on the plastic cloth.

"Lord," Bonnie said, looking at Rhiannon. "What's the matter?"

Bob DiAngelo stumped in. He was frowning again, but he did not seem angry with Rhiannon. Instead, he glared at his wife. "I got her mad at me," he said, "talking to her about things you should be telling her."

"I'm not mad," Rhiannon said. "I'm just tired." She started up the stairs to take a shower and go to bed.

"Hey," her father called after her, and his voice turned her around so that she faced him to hear what he had to say. He stood with his hands on his hips, scowling up at her. "You handle the boys anywhere near as good as you handled that horse," he said in his tough voice, "you'll do okay."

She gave him a tired smile and went on up to her room.

She set her alarm, and the next morning at first light she was slipping out, shortcutting along the railroad tracks, then jogging up Turkey Ridge Road toward Chickie's. If her parents had asked, she would have said she was going to get her bike, and yes, she'd be back in time for Sunday morning breakfast. Be sure to be there, her mother had told her the night before, stopping outside her room door at bedtime. There were bacon and sausage to go with the eggs. The meat had been on sale, and since Bob had stopped drinking Bonnie could afford to buy it. She didn't have to work this Sunday, either. It would be a real family breakfast. Be there.

Rhiannon could have gone to get her bike after breakfast. The truth was, she couldn't wait that long to see how Prince was doing.

By the time she topped the long hill to the Miller farm, she had slowed to a puffing walk, and she went down the gravel lane at a walk. The sun was up, but there was nobody around yet. Ree saw horses in the pasture—Chickie left them out at night in the summertime. They were just dark shapes, for the hollow was still in shadow, and Rhiannon squinted at them as she walked, trying to see which was which. Several of the geldings were gathered over by the fence near the woods—

An airy shape moved beyond them, bright white against the dark trunks of trees, cloud white. Rhiannon stopped where she was, staring. She saw the feathery flow of a long white mane and tail, the high arch of an eager neck, the fine head reaching. Angel was standing there, touching noses with the other horses across the fence.

Rhiannon looked, suddenly aware of early morning's hush, of the muted, contented noises of grazing horses and the clear notes of birds. Angel lifted his lovely head and looked back at her without moving. He knew he had plenty of time to get away from her—but maybe that wasn't why. Maybe he knew she wasn't going to come after him, not this time. After a moment Angel turned and went away at his graceful, floating trot. Within a few strides he disappeared over the lip of the hollow, gone in the woods.

Ree walked quietly down to the shed and looked inside. In the dim light Chickie lay sleeping flat on his back, gently snoring, his chest and belly making the sleeping bag into a softly moving hill. Prince was standing in his stall. His eyes looked bright, he was searching his straw for something to eat, and he stretched his goblin head toward her when he saw her.

EIGHT

"Prince really is getting better, isn't he," Ree said happily to Chickie a few days later.

Chickie had started sleeping in the house again, and Bertha's face had smoothed out. Rhiannon could hear the big woman humming as she baked snicker-doodles. Rhiannon felt like humming herself. Things were finally going right, but it was the first time Ree had dared to say it.

"Heck, yes," Chickie mumbled around some nails stuck in his mouth. "Feet are lots better. Be months before he's really sound, though."

Home from his day's horseshoeing, Chickie was clanking around in the back of his truck, cleaning out the forge. His work jeans were dirty, his shirt was soaked with sweat, and he smelled like a horse— worse than a horse, in fact. Rhiannon didn't mind. She was too happy to mind anything. Every day she could see how Prince had more strength and less pain and was eating more. She could see how the sores were healing. It even looked to her as if the gelding's hollow flanks were filling out some. And Prince had started whickering when she came into the shed.

"No need for you to keep nursemaiding him," Chickie added when he had taken the nails out of his mouth. "You ain't rode Hoss for a while. Why don't you get him out and take a ride?"

"Come with me?"

"Not tonight. Maybe tomorrow. How's your dad?"

"Okay."

"Bring him along up with you again sometime. We'll teach him to ride. How about it?"

Bob DiAngelo on a horse? Not likely, and from Chickie's snaggletoothed grin Ree saw that he knew it. But her father really was okay these days. Things were going better at home, too. Bonnie seemed more relaxed since her husband had stopped drinking. Most of the housework was getting done. Bob DiAngelo did some and made Shawn do some, and Rhiannon did her share when she was home. Also, Rhiannon had heard her parents talking: Bob DiAngelo had put his name in for some sort of job retraining program. Maybe someday he would have a job again.

Rhiannon went and caught Hoss in the pasture. She brought him up to the barn, brushed him and saddled him and rode him up and down the lane, then through the weeds at the edge of the strip site, where her riding had worn a sort of ring around the straggle of scrub pine and thorn trees in the center. Around and around she rode, but all the time she was dreaming of how maybe, someday, when he was all the way better, she would be able to ride Prince.

The gelding had missed her while she was gone. He whinnied at her when she came back to the shed.

A few days later she and Chickie shoveled out his stall, washed it down with disinfectant, and moved him to a stall in the barn with the other horses. Chickie left the bandages off Prince's hooves and started bedding the horse in sawdust. Prince was not a terribly sick horse anymore.

Rhiannon felt glad and sorry. Prince would be well and strong, and he would have the other horses for company. "I guess he doesn't need me anymore," she said doubtfully to Chickie.

Chickie opened his mouth in a grin so wide that the straw he was chewing fell out from between his crooked teeth. "Are you kidding? Look at him!"

Prince had stuck his head through the stall bars, stretching his nose toward her. Rhiannon patted him, feeling the fine, silky, red-brown hair that was starting to grow on his forehead and cheeks.

"He's a real people horse, that one," Chickie said. His grin sagged into an expression that seemed out of place on his broad, homely face. It took Rhiannon a moment to recognize it as sadness. "That's what makes me feel so bad for him."

Rhiannon looked at Chickie, and the big man tried to explain.

"What I mean, there's some as would say them people wasn't really cruel to him. Just ignorant." Chickie sat down on a hay bale and pointed with his straw, teacherlike. "What they say, they didn't beat him or nothing. No marks on him. Nothing like that."

"But they starved him!" Ree protested.

"His teeth was so bad, maybe they thought they was giving him enough to eat and he just couldn't chew it right."

Rhiannon stared. "They let him stand in a dirty stall!" she nearly shouted. "They let him get worms, and they didn't clean his feet, and they let his teeth get that way!"

"What some people say, maybe they didn't know no better."

Ree was so outraged she wanted to scream at Chickie. But she saw the grim, sad look on his face and waited.

"But what I say, they neglected him. You know it and I know it. And to my mind neglect is just like if they beat him. Cruel. They didn't just starve him for food, neither. They starved him for loving."

Rhiannon's mouth came open and she felt a tight ache take hold of her chest. Her hand found the soft place behind Prince's ears and stayed there.

"Look at him," Chickie was saying. "There ain't

105

many horses like him. He just wants to be with people, and he don't hold no grudge for what people done to him. He says you're his person, Rhiannon, and all he wants is to make you happy. When he belonged to them, probably he wanted the same, and all they done was stick him in a corner of the garage."

Ree had a crying feeling in her throat, and until she got rid of it she couldn't speak. She turned her back toward Chickie, patting the horse. "Well," she said finally, huskily, "things are going better now."

"Looks that way."

There was a noise of bike tires outside, then footsteps, a kid's pattering sneakered footsteps. Chickie stuck his straw back in his mouth, heaved himself up, and went to the barn door to take a look. "Yo," he hailed someone.

A young voice said, "Is Ree here?" It was her kid brother, Shawn.

Astonished, she left Prince without even giving him a final pat. She ran to the barn door where Shawn could see her. "Whatcha want?" she demanded.

"You're supposed to come home."

It was early yet. The good, cool evening was just starting. Rhiannon had planned to go for a ride. "How come?" she wanted to know.

"Mom just wants you to come home."

That made no sense. "Mom's at work!"

"No, she ain't. And she's mad because you never left a phone number for up here and she couldn't find it in the book." Shawn spoke importantly. He would say Mom was mad whether she was or not. "She says come home. So come on." Shawn got on his bike. Chickie waved one of his burly hands at Ree and ambled back into the barn. Rhiannon stared, then jogged to her bike.

"Something wrong?" she asked Shawn as they pedaled away.

He shrugged. She would never find out from him if something was wrong or not, or if he knew, or what it might be. Sometimes she thought ten-year-old boys must come from a different planet. Aliens. She tried to get past him on the driveway before they reached the hill down into town, but his bike was as fast as hers and his skinny little legs seemed even stronger and faster. And once he was on the hill she had no hope of catching him. He made gross noises and stayed ahead of her all the way home.

Bonnie DiAngelo was sitting at the kitchen table, waiting, but she didn't look mad. She looked scared, or stunned, and worse than she ever had even after a fourteen-hour day of work. As soon as she saw her mother, Rhiannon knew for sure that something was wrong.

"Mom?"

Bonnie motioned her to a seat on one of the beat-up kitchen chairs and looked at Shawn. "Thanks, honey. You go on back out, now. But not too far."

"Aw, Mom—" Whatever it was Mom had to say, Shawn wanted to hear, too. But Bonnie gave him a look that sent him scuttling, then sat waiting until the boy was out of the yard.

Rhiannon felt her heart beating high in her chest. Whatever it was, it was something bad. Maybe—the railroad trestle—Dad! Where was he?

"Where's Dad?" she blurted at her mother.

"One thing at a time." Bonnie looked at her as if she wasn't really seeing her. "Honey, I don't know what to tell Shawn yet, but I wanted to tell you before you heard it from Lisa or somebody else. Dee's run off. She and Keith ran away together."

At first Rhiannon felt relieved. It was just Deirdre, and she wasn't even dead or anything. Ree felt almost disappointed.

"She called me at work," Bonnie said, so dazed she spoke deadpan, without feeling. "Told me she was with Keith. Said they were going to go someplace and get married. Wouldn't tell me where she was. Then she hung up on me."

Rhiannon felt that something was expected of her. She touched her mother's hand. "Well," she said, "at least they're getting married, not just running off."

Suddenly Bonnie started to cry, startling Ree. What was so bad about getting married? Parents usually acted glad when kids got married, put a picture in the paper and everything. But Bonnie wasn't acting glad, not hardly. Rhiannon stood up so that she could put her arms around her mother. It scared her, seeing Bonnie cry. It scared her whenever her parents cried or anything like that, and suddenly the cold thought of the railroad trestle came to her again, like a punch in the gut. "Mom," she begged, "where's Dad?"

"I came—I came—" Bonnie straightened and reached for a nose tissue, trying to calm down enough so she could talk. "I came home and told him, and he just took off. I don't know where he is."

"I'll go find him," Rhiannon said.

"Ree, no! Stay here with me. It's bad enough—"

Bad enough, Deirdre off somewhere and Dad the same. But Rhiannon wasn't listening. "I have to find him!" she yelled, and she shot out the back door.

Shawn was hanging around in the back alley near the garage. "Go in and stay with Mom," Rhiannon ordered him, and for once he did what he was told.

The car was gone. Her father was probably sitting in some bar, Rhiannon thought harshly, getting drunk. But because she wanted to think otherwise, she turned her bike away from Hoadley, toward the old mine road, where he had gone when he was mad at her. She pedaled hard. The trestle came in sight as she topped the rise, and she peered at it—nothing happening there. She sped down the hill—

The DiAngelo car was pulled up in front of the yellow gate.

Relief made Ree smile a little. Her father was not getting drunk or—or at the trestle. He was taking a walk back the old mine road. She was not sure why it seemed so terribly important to find him, but it still did. She swooped around the gate and sent her bike crunching along as fast as she could on the black gravel road.

She was nearly at the end before she found her father. No Angel that day, no white horse on the hillside, just a middle-aged man walking with slumped shoulders along a shadowy road by the ruins of J. C. Hoadley Co. Coal Mine 27.

He turned when he heard her coming, and as she stopped the bike she found that she didn't know what to say to him.

"You heard about Deirdre?"

She nodded. He stood looking at her. "Dad," she burst out, "please come home."

He stopped looking at her, and for a minute he didn't move. Then with short steps he walked forward so that he stood at her side. She turned her bike, and very slowly they both walked back toward the house. There was a prickly silence. Rhiannon felt she had to say something.

"I'm glad you're not drinking," she blurted.

"Don't tempt me." Bob DiAngelo did not look up or smile. "Your mom crying?"

"Some. Dad, what's so terrible about Deirdre getting married?"

His head jerked up, and for a moment the glare of his eyes under his dark, scowling brows made her afraid. She said, "I mean, like, I know she did it without asking you and everything. But—"

Bob DiAngelo said, "She might as well have killed herself and had it done with."

Rhiannon felt as if a cold hand was squeezing her heart. She stopped pushing her bike along the road. She couldn't say anything.

"All the waste," her father said fiercely, very angry, but at Deirdre, not at Ree. "Everything your mother and I put into her. Everything she could have been. Gone."

Rhiannon started walking again, head down over her bike, trying to figure it out. Deirdre wasn't on drugs. Deirdre had never even been in any kind of trouble that Rhiannon knew of. Timidly Ree asked, "Is she pregnant?"

"Maybe. What does it matter? If she ain't now, she soon will be." Bob DiAngelo's voice sounded as harsh as the coal brickle underfoot. "She'll be in a big rush to have a kid, maybe two or three, and her so-called husband will work at this job and that, and they'll move from one crummy apartment to another with never enough money for anything. No regular doctoring for the kids, no good clothes, no nothing. After a while he'll leave her, or she'll leave him, and her without even a high school diploma, no chance at a decent job, little kids to take care of. . . ."

"How do you know it's going to happen that way?" Rhiannon protested.

"I just know. She's digging herself into a hole so deep, she'll never be able to climb out of it. She'll end up on welfare, or asking your mom and me for help, or both."

Rhiannon asked, "But how can you say for sure that it's wrong? I mean, Keith might be real nice. He—"

"I don't care if he's a prince on a white horse!" Bob DiAngelo's voice rose to a shout. "It's wrong because it's put together half-assed to start with, and that's why it's going to fall apart, Rhiannon!" He glared at her in fury for a moment, then turned and hit one of the trees along the road, banged it with his fist so hard that his knuckles started to bleed, then leaned against it and put his head down as if he wanted to cry.

Rhiannon stood still, scared, but when her father started to talk again his voice was very low and calm, as if the anger had all left him.

"Ree, listen. I seen it happen so often. My sister Linda—there's things you don't know about her. She's been through hell. Or your mother. She wanted to be a teacher, and she could've been a good one. She had the grades, she could've gone to state college. But her and me was young fools, we decided we was going to get married. I had a job waiting for me at the steel mill, I went straight out of high school into the mill, and she had babies and never finished her education. So now she's working for chickenshit in the shirt factory and putting up with the crap the foreman—"

Rhiannon hated to hear her father talking as if

marrying her mother had been a mistake. She inter-rupted, "How could you know the mill was going to close!"

"Dammit, Ree, would you just listen?" Her father turned and grabbed her by the shoulders, scowling into her eyes. "It's not just the rotten job. It's that—she could've been something. She never— She's never been really happy. There's a time for things. She could've gone to school, but she married me and had babies instead, and by the time the babies were old enough she felt like it was too late, she couldn't do it no more. Even if I was still working it wouldn't make no difference. But we thought things would be better for you kids—and now, dammit, can't you see, it's happening—"

Her father let go of her and stood taking several deep breaths, his eyes glaring off over her head somewhere, as if he saw something he could barely face, as if he could barely say what it was. His voice went low and dead.

"It's happening all over again."

Bob DiAngelo started down the road, walking fast this time, as if something was after him. Rhiannon had to hurry to catch up with him.

"You kids," he said numbly as she panted along by his side. "We pinned it all on you kids. She read books to you. Every week, to the library for more books. She always made you speak good grammar." Made Bob DiAngelo do the same, Rhiannon knew, though her father's grammar always started to slip when he was upset. He said, "She seen to it that you done your best in school, and I just figured I'd work some more overtime and bring in the money, send you to college someday. Should've paid more attention to Deirdre and her boyfriends early on."

He sounded very bitter. Rhiannon didn't look at him. She mumbled, "It's getting dark."

We'll soon be home, he should have said, but instead he said, "Rhiannon, don't you see, that's why I worry so much about you going off the way you do. I should've worried about Dee, but I didn't. She was our first, we made lots of mistakes with her. I don't want to make the same ones with you, or you won't have a snowball's chance in hell of getting out of here."

"Out of here?"

"Out of this hole we've got ourselves dug into. Hell, this whole place is a hole. Hoadley is just one big empty black coal hole."

He was sober but his words sounded drunk. Rhiannon shivered. She was glad to see the yellow gate ahead, and the streetlights and row houses beyond it. "Dad," she said suddenly, "whenever you go off like that, I get scared."

He stopped and looked at her in the pale light from the street. "Scared of what?"

She wanted to say "Nothing," but something made her tell the truth. She felt she owed it to him since he had leveled with her. She said, "Scared you might kill yourself."

His face went white with shock, but he didn't yell at her, the way he would have if it had been close to true. He said, "God." Then he said, "Baby, I'm sorry."

"It's not your fault."

"Yes, it is. I was killing myself the slow way, drinking, and you knew it. Smart kid."

They walked on. After a minute Rhiannon's father said, "I'll never go off that way again."

Shabby old mine town row houses, plain two-story boxes, one very much the same as the others. One of them was home.

Ree on her bike and her father in the car, they got there at the same time. When they went in, Bonnie DiAngelo was still sitting at the table. Her husband stood looking at her with no expression on his face, but she stared back at him in surprise.

"I thought you'd be drinking," she said.

He shook his head. "Me and Ree been talking. Any word from the cops?"

"Nothing."

"She's probably in another state by now."

"I guess. You want some coffee?"

"Yeah. Thanks. Where's Shawn?"

"Going to bed."

Rhiannon said, "I'm going up, too."

"Goodnight, kid," said her father. "Hey—thanks for coming to get me."

NINE

"Policeman, policeman, do your duty!
Here comes Didi, American beauty!
She can wiggle, she can waggle, she can do the
  twist!
Bet you any money she can't do this:
Turn around, touch the ground,
Leave town. . . ."

The little girls were jumping rope out front. Rhiannon could hear them faintly through the walls.

All night there had been no word about Deirdre, though Bob and Bonnie DiAngelo had sat up waiting, and that morning Rhiannon felt she should stay home from the barn. So there she was in the house, hanging around and nearly jumping out of her skin with wanting to go see Prince. Her father and mother had stayed home too. They were drink-

116

ing coffee at the kitchen table, not doing anything. Grandma Phillips and Grandma DiAngelo were sitting at opposite ends of the sofa, ignoring each other. Even Shawn was in the house, in his room. Everybody was so quiet it was as if Deirdre had died, except that nobody came bringing casseroles.

About midmorning Rhiannon noticed Lisa Toth standing on the front sidewalk. Up early, for Lisa. Rhiannon guessed Lisa didn't want to knock on the door in case the DiAngelos didn't want company. She watched for a while as Lisa pretended she was just hanging around, then went outside to talk with her.

"Hi," she said.

"Oh, hi." For a minute Lisa tried to act as if there was nothing on her mind, then she gave it up. "You hear from Deirdre yet?" she pounced.

"Not since yesterday."

"Cops didn't find her?"

"No."

The little girls and their jump rope, two enders with a long rope and one jumper in the middle, had moved to the sidewalk in front of the next house. The enders were chanting,

"Fudge, fudge, call the judge!
Didi's having a ba-by!
Wrap it up in tissue paper,
Send it down the elevator. . . ."

"Wow. Maybe she's married already," said Lisa dreamily, with the same glow in her eyes as she got when she was looking at Bucky Miller.

Rhiannon frowned at her friend. She didn't like the feeling she was getting about Lisa.

"You knew all about it," she said.

"Well, you would've too, if you wasn't out at that horse farm all the time."

She hadn't seen much of Lisa since she had started going to Chickie's place, and especially not since she had been taking care of Prince. Suddenly she noticed that Lisa was wearing eye shadow in the daytime. No big deal, but Lisa had on so much it looked silly. Plum Passion eyelids and cutoff shorts.

"She told you?"

"Not really. But everybody knew her and Keith was real serious." Lisa started to smile a misty-eyed smile.

"Cinderella, dressed in yellow,
Went upstairs to kiss a fellow,
Made a mistake and kissed a snake!"

Raising her voice against the little-girl singsong, Rhiannon protested, "Lisa, wouldja wake up? Why didn't you tell my parents or somebody?"

Lisa's dewy-eyed gaze widened into surprise. "Are you crazy?"

"Well, you could've at least told me."

"So was you gonna tell them?"

Rhiannon wasn't sure what she would have done. Maybe Lisa had done her a favor by not telling her anything. But she still felt funny about her friend. She looked at Lisa for a minute, then turned and went back into the house. The little girls with the jump rope were spinning it fast, chanting about babies.

"Girls, boys, twins, triplets!
Girls, boys, twins, triplets!"

Rhiannon shut the door on the voices.

For the next several hours she did housework furiously, a sort of penance, as if she had done something wrong. She changed beds and laundered the sheets. She cleaned the kitchen, scrubbing the sink and countertops her dad had not been wiping very often, then getting down on her hands and knees and scrubbing the baseboards and floor. She was so busy scrubbing that she didn't want to stop for lunch, and none of the adults felt hungry. Shawn was the only one who ate. Meanwhile Rhiannon cleaned the bathroom, then routed her grandmothers by vacuuming the living room, and she was getting ready to start washing windows when her mother stopped her.

"Ree, don't work so hard. You're only twelve years old." Bonnie saw the astonished look her daughter was giving her and answered it with a tired smile. "I know, I keep telling you to do this, do that. You're so big and act so grown-up I keep forgetting how young you really are. Here, be a kid for a change. Go down the drugstore or someplace and get yourself something." Her mother handed her a dollar.

Rhiannon felt her mouth sag open. Treats were unheard-of since her father had lost his job. From his seat at the kitchen table, Bob DiAngelo gave a dark chuckle.

"What a screwy day," he said. Seeing his daughter looking at him, he shrugged and nodded. "Sure, hon. Go on."

Rhiannon pocketed the dollar and went out, but she didn't want to go into the ThriftiDrug. Lisa was likely to be there. Ree felt sort of mad at Lisa.

She walked around Hoadley for a while, looking in the Hoadley store, the run-down general store that used to be the company store. She knew before she started that the dollar wasn't enough to buy anything she really wanted or could use, just candy and stuff. She looked in the store anyway, then thought of going down to the ThriftiDrug, Lisa or no Lisa, to look at the magazines and see how much the *Horse Illustrated* was. But she knew it was more than a dollar. The firehouse clock said 2:30. What a long day.

She bought a bag of cheap candy, the kind that's mostly sugar, at a corner store, then home, eating a box of Nerds on the way.

The next day Bonnie went back to work and caught it from both her bosses for missing a day, Shawn went back to bike riding on the bony piles, and Rhiannon went back to the Miller farm. She stopped and looked at her father on her way out the door.

"Come with me?" she offered. Bob DiAngelo shook his head.

"I have to hang around in case the phone rings. Thanks anyway, kid."

Coasting down the Miller lane on her bike, Rhiannon saw a strange new horse standing by itself in a small section of pasture near the barn, fenced off with electric wire. It was a tall, very thin horse with straight, slim legs and a long, handsome head and neck. Maybe it was a thoroughbred. Where could Chickie have gotten it?

The horse was watching her as she came nearer, small ears pricked forward, and then it whickered and headed toward her at a fast, limping trot.

Rhiannon gasped. It was Prince, without his blanket, without the bandages on his feet, outside to greet her for the first time.

"Prince!" Rhiannon was so surprised and happy that she nearly forgot to turn off the electric fence before she touched it. But she remembered in time, turned the power off at the box and went in at the gate to hug the big horse. Prince laid his nose on her shoulder and nibbled her hair. She stroked him. She couldn't believe how good he looked and felt. There was hair growing all over him, dark red-brown hair full of golden lights and silky-smooth to the touch.

"He hollered for you yesterday," said a voice behind her. Chickie was standing at the gate with his leather apron slung over his T-shirted shoulder, ready to go to work. He must have had the apron in the house to mend it or clean it. "Watched for you all day, hollered when he thought you was coming."

Rhiannon hugged Prince around the neck again. "I had to stay home," she said.

Chickie nodded and didn't ask any questions. He looked thoughtfully at Prince. "Bet he'll ride English," he remarked, "when he's better."

"He looks like he might've been, like, a show horse," said Ree. "You know, like, a jumper or something."

"Or a hunter. Maybe. He needs lots of rest and good feeding before we put a saddle on him, though." Chickie's glance shifted to Ree. "Bert's home today to keep an eye on you, so why don't you try riding some of the others besides Hoss. Try Rowdy, only just don't hold him too tight in the mouth. Or Punky." Chickie flapped one big hand at her and went off. In a minute she heard his truck chugging up the lane.

It was different, riding Rowdy. He did everything faster than Hoss. He even walked faster, and he kept his head up, looking around. Rhiannon walked him around the house and barnyard, then down to the woods and back, around and around the strip site, then up the lane and back, before she got used to him. Finally she started to trust him and relaxed. Then she trotted him, feeling the difference between Rowdy's willing trot and Hoss's sluggish jog, and a prickle of excitement ran up her spine. She walked him again for a little while, then loped him up the lane. No need to kick this horse to keep him going. With every stride Rowdy went a little faster. Rhiannon felt wind lifting her hair and an I-did-it thrill lifting her head. She was with the horse, as if she was part of the horse, and seemingly all by itself her body rocked to his stride. Rowdy wanted to speed up into a gallop, but Rhiannon wasn't ready for that yet. She had a good grip on the reins to keep the horse from going any faster. She and Rowdy cantered up the lane through locust thicket, sumac, and old apple trees—

Somebody was walking at the side of the lane, and Rowdy spooked.

The horse swerved like a car on ice, his hindquarters spinning out and away from what had frightened him. Sitting deep in the saddle with her heels down, the way Chickie had taught her, Rhiannon felt her hands and legs checking the horse before she had time to think. Before she fully knew what had happened it was all over, and she was still on top of Rowdy. Then she was scared, but also excited, and her lips came apart in a breathless smile. She'd done it! She'd stayed on a shying horse.

The person at the side of the lane had stopped walking. It was Bucky, with a piece of chrome something-or-other from the junkyard in his hand, standing and looking at her. He put the car part down in the grass and weeds by his feet, then straightened up and looked at her some more. There was an odd, intent expression on his face.

"C'mere a minute," he said.

"Huh?"

"C'mere, Rhiannon. I want to show you something."

It was the way he said her name that made her get down off Rowdy and come over to him, leading the horse by the reins. She had no idea what Bucky wanted, except that it must be important. In a way, it was. When she stopped in front of him, Bucky took her head gently between his big hands, stooped a little and kissed her on the mouth.

Nobody had ever done that to her before. And it felt so good it seemed to stop her heart.

Bucky was a good kisser. He had been practicing on somebody, and he wasn't nervous, and he took his time. One of his hands moved around to the back of her head, where his fingers nestled into her hair. The other slipped down her neck and around to the middle of her back. And what he was doing to her mouth made her feel hot and excited clear down to her toes.

And scared. When the hand on her back nudged her closer to him, she stiffened against it and pulled her head away from his.

Bucky's face came back into focus, staring down at her. Breathing fast, she looked at him. He was good-looking, a real hunk. Lisa and half the girls in Hoadley were running after him. Rhiannon had never thought about him except as a friend. But the way he was looking at her made her think differently.

"Tie that horse someplace," he said in a strange, quiet voice, "and I'll show you some more things." His hand moved softly down her back. The other one slipped to her shoulder.

She wanted to. Her whole body felt good just because he had kissed her. If her father knew, he would get mad and hit her. So what. Her father had been hassling her and checking up on her ever since she had started coming to the Miller place, so why not give him something to hassle about? Serve him right if she did start running around with Bucky! And Lisa would die when she found out.

Lisa in her purple eyeshadow, dreamy about Deirdre and Keith. . . .

Rhiannon jerked away from Bucky's hands and stepped back, suddenly furious at him and the whole world without knowing why except that he had scared her. She was more scared than ever, and so mad she wanted to slap Bucky across the face. She wished he would laugh and say he was just kidding around with her, so she would have an excuse. But he wasn't laughing, or even smiling.

"I never asked you to show me anything!" she yelled at him, and she started back down toward the barn, leading Rowdy. After a few steps she got scared that Bucky would follow her, so she stopped, not looking behind her, and scrambled onto the horse. Couldn't even mount right because she thought he might be watching—the thought made her face turn red, but she didn't look to see if he was. She sent Rowdy trotting down the lane, back toward the barn, bouncing around in the saddle because she was too rattled to ride right.

Getting the saddle and bridle off the horse and brushing him dry calmed her down somewhat. After she turned Rowdy out in the pasture again, she got Prince in, tied him in his stall and started grooming him with the softest brush. Prince didn't need it, but she needed to do it. Prince was her friend, she could hug him and he wouldn't do anything weird. She liked Bucky as a friend, too—that was what made her so upset. She didn't know how she was going to face him again. If she could just hate him, it would be easier.

"Hey, Ree."

She jumped at the voice behind her, already knowing who it was, already edging away before she turned around. Bucky, of course.

"Go away," she said.

"Hey, I ain't done nothing bad to you. Nothing you didn't like. What's the matter?" He was keeping his distance. She relaxed a little and looked straight at him. He wasn't laughing at her now, either.

"Nothing," Rhiannon said.

"I'm sorry I come on to you so fast," said Bucky. "I mean, I could of at least asked you for a date or something."

"I don't think I'm allowed."

He looked hard at her. "Cripes, you can't date yet? How old are you, fourteen?"

She felt her face go red. How was she going to tell him she was only twelve? She wanted to lie and say she was thirteen, anyway. She really would be thirteen in a few weeks. But what was the use of saying that? She didn't want him kissing her again. Or did she?

She hadn't answered. "The way you looked when you was riding that horse," Bucky said after a minute, "I thought you was fifteen, anyway."

"I'm twelve."

"Jeez," Bucky breathed. "You're just a little kid."

Rhiannon was mad at him all over again. "I am not!" she shouted.

"I didn't mean it that way. I just meant—"

"Just forget it, Bucky." Suddenly tired, Rhiannon turned back to brushing Prince. She didn't want to hear any more.

"I got no damn business," Bucky said. "Nice kid like you. Ree, I'm really sorry."

She didn't answer or look at him. After a minute she heard him walk away and out the barn door.

Riding home, Rhiannon turned off Turkey Ridge Road and took the railroad shortcut, walking her bike across the bridge that overpassed 27 Street. She dawdled, reading the many graffiti. The inside of the bridge was more obscene than the outside, she noted. There was a crude picture resembling a cactus but meant to be something else, and there were all the old worn-out bad words. Over everything, in garish orange spray paint, someone had recently added, "Love Stinks."

At home, there was no news from Deirdre or about her.

TEN

"The thing is, is that people will just breed for the heck of it," Chickie said. "People are ignorant. They get the idea it would be cute to have a foal, and they don't think about that cute foal getting sold for meat."

He was sitting on the porch glider after work, having a beer, looking down in the pasture at all the horses and trying to explain to Rhiannon how he came to have so many. In the past week Rhiannon had ridden Punky, Cat, and Butterscotch. Cameron was ridable but might be too much of a handful for her, Chickie thought, and the others mostly were not ridable. He was starting to explain why.

"So they breed the mare, and they have a cute foal. And that cute foal is going to grow up into a horse no use to anybody, maybe just plain dangerous unless it's broke right. But they don't know how to do it right. They think they got some idea because they been riding horses, but they don't know half of it, the work they got to do and the time involved. And of course they're not going to spend money and take that colt to a professional trainer. Heck, no. So the horse ends up green broke."

Chickie took a long swig of his beer. "Green broke?" Rhiannon asked.

"About half trained. Like a person who maybe dropped out of school and never learned no special skills. You can get on the horse and it'll go, but it's no pleasure to ride. It don't know how to come on the bit or yield to leg, it ain't got no good manners or good gaits, maybe it does things it shouldn't, like run back to the barn, and the rider don't correct it. Maybe the rider is a kid, don't make the horse do what it's supposed to. Long as they're getting a horseback ride, they don't care what the horse does."

Rhiannon scowled at this way of talking about kids. "So if they're happy," she argued, "what does it matter?"

"It matters cause the horse is useless. Nobody ever thinks about the horse. Sooner or later the kid grows up, goes away from home. Or if it's a girl, most often she loses interest in the horse after a while, gets interested in boys instead." Chickie grinned at Rhiannon. She didn't grin back. "Maybe there's a divorce, or a move, or somebody loses a job. Whatever reason, sooner or later they have to get rid of the horse. Then they find out nobody wants to buy a green-broke horse."

"Couldn't somebody buy it and train it right?"

Chickie finished his beer and set the can down on the porch floor before he answered.

"Older the horse is, the harder it is to train. But sometimes it happens that way. Maybe the horse is real nice-looking, and somebody decides to take the trouble. Or the horse is registered, and somebody buys it because of that. Mostly, though, people want to buy *made* horses. Well, think about it. Would you buy something that needed fixed before it would work right?"

"Maybe if it was real cheap."

"Now, that's the thing."

Chickie sounded as if he was going to talk some more, but he didn't right away. He got up and walked down the porch steps, down the sloping yard to the pasture fence, and he leaned on a fence post and looked at his horses. Rhiannon followed and stood by him. When Chickie spoke, his booming voice had gotten very quiet.

"So they sell their baby very cheap. Their baby foal that they loved and raised. But the person who buys it finds out that it's got bad habits, it's too much trouble to retrain, and they decide to get rid of it, but who the heck are they gonna sell it to? And why should they advertise and ask around and end up selling it for three hundred bucks when they can take it to the stock auction and get six hundred for it for meat?"

"Oh," Rhiannon said in a small voice.

"Yeah. Ree, you should see them places. I mean, I hope you never do. Turns your stomach. Thing is, people take better care of horses they pay good money for. What I've seed—you wouldn't believe it. The horses that comes into them places, some of them look like Prince when he first come here."

"So that's why—where—"

Sunset glow lay over the pasture, so that the horses grazing amid daisies and dandelions seemed all like palominos, like golden horses out of a peaceful dream. It was hard to believe they had once been abused, neglected, or starved.

"A lot of them come from there," Chickie said. "Hoss come from there, and Butterscotch, and Rowdy. Them was the first I got, and I retrained them good. Toby and Cricket come from there but I never got around to training them. Bert made me quit going then. It tore me up too much, I wanted to bring them all home."

After a while Rhiannon asked, "What about, like, Punky?"

"Punky I just plain bought. He's a good horse. Cameron I bought off the track. He had a blown tendon, just needed rest, but he's real high strung, like most of them thoroughbreds that's been raced. Cat has arthritis, was give to me by a friend. Lena they was gonna sell for meat. She was a good jumper once but she ain't been handled right, she's useless any more even if she didn't have hoof problems, which she does. Jingles is just a kid's pony ain't never been broke right, like most of them little ponies. See how thick his neck is?" Chickie sounded amused. "That's from pulling the bit away from little kids. Good for nothing but to lead around. Word gets around after a while, people brought him here and I took him. Shiloh I got pretty much the same way. But none of the bunch of them was as bad off as Prince."

Chickie was silent as they both looked at Prince for a while. The gelding stood dozing in his private pasture, golden sunset light touching him. "I bet he put on fifty pounds already," Chickie said. "He might have some thoroughbred in him, but he's nice and calm, he don't fuss it off like Cameron would. Next week you can start leading him around the place, give him a little exercise."

"You think—you think I'm going to be able to ride him, ever?"

Chickie looked straight at Rhiannon. "Sure thing," he said. "Even if we have to start him from scratch. Which don't seem likely. But you know you're going to have to wait till he's really better. Maybe next spring."

"That's okay," Rhiannon said.

Chickie nodded and went into the barn to feed. Horses started drifting up pasture at the sound of the grain being scooped into the buckets. Ree stayed where she was, leaning against the shed wall, watching them. Sunset had turned to dusk, and the horses weren't golden dreams anymore, but shadows, dark horses climbing a dark hill faintly starred with daisies. All of them were coming up except Tiffany, the old swaybacked gray mare, who was always last. Still grazing in the bottom of the hollow, she looked ghostly white in the twilight. Something moved, and she raised her wise old head to look—

Rhiannon gasped. There was another white horse standing beyond Tiffany, at the edge of the woods.

"Chickie," she called softly.

"What say?" he bellowed from the barn.

"Chickie! C'mere! It's Angel."

Bearlike but quick, he lumbered to her side. She pointed. "Down by the woods."

"That's Tiffany," Chickie said.

"I know that's Tiffany!" Rhiannon was annoyed. "Look further down. Right outside—" She blinked, puzzled. She had not seen Angel leave, but the twilight seemed to be playing tricks on her. The Arabian was gone. "Well, he was there a minute ago, right outside the fence!"

"You sure?" Chickie was smiling. She heard it in his voice.

"I know what I saw!" she complained. "Angel was down there."

"Well, I ain't never seed him since the day he run away, but you see him all the time!" Chickie was grinning broadly and chuckling to himself. "I got to say, sometimes I think you're just doing it to pester me."

134

"I saw him!" She punched Chickie lightly in his hard, ample belly, then thought of something. "How did you get Angel, anyway?"

"Same old story." Chickie stopped chuckling and turned back toward the barn; Ree followed him. "People raised him from a colt, didn't train him right, let him run wild, and he got too hot for them to handle. They had him gelded, but it was too late for that to do much good. I took him because nobody else would. Turned out he was too wild for me to hold, either."

"What about Tiffany? Where did you get her?"

"Didn't nobody ever tell you about Tiffany?" Chickie turned toward her and set down the buckets of feed he was carrying. "She was a carnival horse. One of the last of them diving horses. Maybe the very last."

"Diving horse?"

"Used to be a big thing. The horse would dive off a tower, thirty, forty feet high into a big tub of water. Tiffany done it most all her life. Never learned nothing else, not to ride, drive, nothing. When the act went broke they was going to put her down. Seems there ain't no retirement home for old carnival horses."

Rhiannon helped Chickie hang the water buckets and feed buckets in the stalls and let in the horses, Prince first, then the others, one by one, until each stall showed a long head dipping into the grain, shadowy in the dim light of a single bulb.

"Old Tiffany," Chickie added, "she must be thirty, thirty-five years old by now. All crippled up, but she still bosses the bunch of them."

Tiffany had a white face. Some of the others had white foreheads, blazes, stars. Rhiannon watched them eat, and all the time flickers of white were darting through her head. A silvery mare going off a high tower. Flash of something flying as if it had white wings. The cloudlike floating of a long, wild mane and tail.

Prince had no white markings. She patted him and told him to enjoy his grain, then rode home, looking down from the ridge for a glint of white in the nightfall, half expecting to hear hooves under the trees, then to see something large and beautiful leap and fly.

She got home late, but the DiAngelo house was in such an uproar that no one noticed or scolded her for riding her bike home in the near dark. Deirdre had called, sobbing, and asked her father to come and get her. She would meet him in a McDonald's in Hagerstown. Bob DiAngelo was on his way out the back door when Rhiannon was coming in. Bonnie and Shawn were trailing after him, both talking at once, and it took Rhiannon half a minute to figure out why her mother was home from work and what was going on. Her father was hugging her for no reason except that he felt good.

"I saw Angel again, Dad!" she yelled after him when he let go of her and went.

It was a strange thing for her to say. She had never told her family about Angel.

"It's, like, every time I see him, things get better," she confided to Lisa the next morning.

Lisa had been hanging around on the sidewalk in front of the house again. News travels fast in a small town. Everybody knew Deirdre was home and sleeping in after the long, late drive. Bob DiAngelo was up as early as ever, drinking his coffee, bleary-eyed, but Deirdre seemed to be in no hurry to wake up, and Rhiannon was waiting in the living room. Even if she wasn't curious to see what was going to happen, which she was, Ree didn't feel she could go to Chickie's. Her mother had found a ride to work, leaving the car in case her husband needed it, and Rhiannon thought she'd better stick around in case her father needed her for something. There were times families were supposed to stay close, and this felt like one of them. But it was boring, waiting to be useful, and she was glad to see Lisa. She went out right away to talk to her.

"Like, Angel made me meet Chickie, and everything," she explained to Lisa in awed tones. She was glad to have a chance to talk this out to somebody. It was not the sort of thing she could tell her father or mother, especially not when their heads were full of Deirdre. "Then we saw him the time we found Dad walking down there and he wasn't drinking or anything. Then the next time I saw him, Prince started to get better. Then I didn't see him again till last night, and when I got home Deirdre had called."

Lisa listened impatiently and complained, "What's the horse got to do with Deirdre?"

"Nothing! I just mean—it's weird."

"*You're* weird," Lisa accused.

"I'm just saying what happened!"

Lisa wanted to hear about Deirdre, so she didn't argue. "What about Dee?" she asked instead.

Rhiannon retorted, "What about her?"

"She's home, right? How come?"

Ree blinked. It seemed to her that Lisa knew as much as she did. "She called Dad and asked him to come get her."

"But how come? Did Keith leave her? Was he mean to her? Did he slap her around or something, or do drugs, or try to make her turn tricks, or what?"

Rhiannon stared at her friend. "Good grief," she said, and she turned and went back into the house.

Her father had finished his first cup of coffee and was huddled over his second. Rhiannon sat down at the table across from him. "Dad," she asked him with a direct look, "did Dee tell you anything on the way home last night?"

"Just that married life wasn't what she expected." Bob DiAngelo seemed bitterly amused. Rhiannon saw a tight-lipped smile under his dark mustache. "Keith seemed to expect her to cook and do dishes and laundry while he hunted for work, or else get a job herself."

"Is that all?"

Bob DiAngelo lost his smile. "What do you mean, is that all? Don't tell me there's rumors going around already."

Rhiannon didn't answer. After a moment her father said, "As far as I know, it's the way I told you. Probably she thought Keith should take her out to dinner and dancing and make love to her all the time." Her father's voice had gotten harsh. "Couldn't see why she should have to work."

Deirdre was finally out of bed. Rhiannon could hear her sloshing around in the bathtub upstairs. There would be the hum of a hairdryer for a while, then a long silence while she dressed and applied makeup and curling iron, and finally Deirdre would come down with every curl of her perm in place, just in time to eat a meal someone else had made.

"No wonder," Rhiannon said. "She never did any work around here."

"Don't you bad-mouth your sister," said Bob DiAngelo sharply.

Rhiannon said nothing. She knew better than to answer back when her father spoke that way, but she felt irritated and jealous. It seemed to her that Deirdre was always the favorite daughter. If she, Rhiannon, got herself into trouble, would her father defend her? Should she try it and see?

Sourly she got up and fixed breakfast. Just when the fried potatoes and eggs were ready, Deirdre came down, cool and crisp, looking like a beauty contest winner, every curl in place, as Rhiannon had known she would.

Ree clunked a plate of food down in front of her sister, trying to think of something mean she could say in front of her father without being punished. And Deirdre looked up at her scowling younger sister and suddenly crumpled into tears. Her mascara ran down her face, and the brownish tears dropped onto her eggs. Deirdre sat without moving, not even to push the plate aside, not even to put a napkin to her eyes, just sat there sobbing.

Rhiannon went and got her the box of tissue, then stood at Dee's side with her mouth open, not knowing what else to do.

"Go get your breakfast, Ree." Bob DiAngelo was eating his, with a look as if his stomach hurt him. "No use letting your eggs get cold."

Rhiannon ate, though she didn't feel hungry anymore. Deirdre stopped sobbing, blew her nose and wiped her face, but didn't eat. After a while Rhiannon said to her, "Dee."

"What." Her voice came out sounding as if she had a bad cold.

"What do you want me to tell people when they ask me why you're back?"

She started crying again, but talked through it. "I got . . . homesick, is all! I just . . . wanted . . . to come home."

Bob DiAngelo took his plate to the sink and rinsed the egg off it, then came back and took Dee's untouched breakfast. "Come on, Dee." His voice was gentle but tough enough not to make her cry. "Get yourself together. We got to get going."

"Where are you going?" Rhiannon asked her father.

Deirdre lifted her reddened, teary face, and her lips curled back. "None of your business!" she flared at her sister.

But Bob DiAngelo said, "Yes, it is her business, Deirdre. What you do affects her, one way or another." To Rhiannon he said, "We're going to the doctor to see if we can get her some help."

Deirdre put a cold dishrag to her face and fixed herself up somewhat. Then she and her father went out.

Rhiannon watched as they walked to the rusting-out car, and watched as her father drove away. She wasn't sure what sort of help her father meant, but she no longer felt jealous of Deirdre for getting all this attention. Deirdre was in trouble. And trouble meant something so bad that parents wouldn't get mad at you because they were afraid you couldn't take it.

And they felt like it was partly their fault, for not training you right. And they were afraid you would end up being, like, sold for meat.

Rhiannon shivered and started into a housework binge. She would stay home all day and make cooked meals for her brother and make something good for supper.

ELEVEN

Rhiannon took Lisa up to the Miller place to see Prince.

She was so proud of the horse she had to show somebody. And it was all still Deirdre, Deirdre, Deirdre at home. Deirdre was on pills to keep her from crying all the time, so now she slept all the time, and didn't want to go out, and wouldn't come to the phone even when her friends called her. She wasn't pregnant, so there was no need to have anything to do with Keith. He would be notified when Deirdre's marriage was legally over. Bob DiAngelo had found a cheap lawyer to take care of it, and he was worrying about getting the money to pay him, and he shook his head when Rhiannon asked him to come see the horses with her. When he wasn't hunting odd jobs he was hanging around the house, worried about leaving Deirdre alone for too long.

"Hi, Dee," Rhiannon had said, passing her sister's closed door the night before. Nobody had answered, but she pushed the door open anyway. By the hall light she could see Deirdre lying on her bed in the darkened room, staring up at the shadows on the cracked ceiling.

"Hi," Rhiannon said.

"Drop dead," said Deirdre.

"You ought to get out of this room sometimes," said Ree. "You want to come see the horses with me tomorrow?"

With sudden energy Deirdre sat up and threw a paperback book at her. Rhiannon stood still and let it bang against her forehead. "That didn't hurt," she said. "Want to try another?"

Deirdre grabbed another from the stack of teen romances at her bedside, cocked it to throw, then dropped it and started to cry. Rhiannon went over and sat on the bed beside her.

"You going back to Vo-Tech this fall?"

"I guess." Deirdre dried up quickly. She was tired of crying, and the pills made her numb.

"What course are you going to take?"

"I don't really care."

"Well, what do you think I should take?"

"I could—" Deirdre stopped saying she couldn't care less and stared at Ree. "Good grief, you don't have to decide for another three years yet."

"Well, I just want to be something, is all. Do something. Not like—" Rhiannon stopped herself.

"Not like me?" Deirdre asked.

"Not like all the other girls around here."

Deirdre was not fooled. "Get out," she said, meaning it. "Get lost. Go away. Leave me alone." So Rhiannon had gone.

She had to mention Bucky, the next day, to talk Lisa into going to see her horse with her. Lisa agreed, but she would not ride her bike, so after an early supper the girls hiked up the hill the back way, down the old mine road and up the trail Ree knew from her horseback riding. Rhiannon liked that way better than walking up the road, because the woods were cool and breezy even in the August heat. But Lisa complained about stones in her shoes, and twigs, and scratchy things.

"My legs are getting all scratched up!"

Rhiannon eyed Lisa's smooth legs, tanned from lying around the pool. Her own legs were a patriotic red, white, and blue. Red from scratches, blue from bruises, and white from wearing jeans to ride.

"Aw, maaan, my arms are getting scratched up, too!" Lisa moaned.

"You'll live," Rhiannon told her.

At the pasture fence the heat met them like something solid, but it was a sunny, sweet-smelling heat, full of the scents of flowers and leaves. Coming up along the pasture line, Rhiannon saw Queen Anne's lace and purple ironweed blossoms. She stroked the plumy tops of field grass as she passed them, but Lisa wailed, "Something's biting me!"

"He won't eat much," Ree snapped.

"Rhiannon, this better be good!"

Ree didn't answer. She led the way out of the weeds, around the shed and over to the small pasture where Prince was kept. As soon as the horse saw her he whickered and trotted over to her. His hooves hadn't yet grown back into their proper shape after being trimmed for thrush, but he wasn't limping anymore. His head rode steady at the trot, and the gait was long, strong, and reaching.

"He's nice," Lisa said doubtfully.

"He's *super*," Ree corrected her.

She turned off the electric fence, put a lead rope on Prince and got him out. He offered his head to Rhiannon to be scratched, then swung it curiously toward Lisa. She backed away.

"Pat him," said Ree. "He likes you."

Lisa touched the horse with her fingertips and started to smile. Rhiannon tied Prince to a fence post and went to get the brushes. She handed Lisa the soft one. Prince was covered with hair now, silky hair the dark red-brown color of polished cherry wood. His mane, still growing in, was the same color, fine and wispy and so short that it stood straight up, nodding when he moved.

"He looks like somebody gave him a Mohawk," said Lisa, giggling.

"Just don't go putting purple stripes in it." Rhiannon brushed Prince carefully but firmly. On the other side of the horse from her, Lisa gave lazy swipes with the soft brush from time to time. "He's got spots," Lisa said.

"Huh?" Rhiannon came around and looked where Lisa was pointing. In the slanting sunset light, Prince's smooth hindquarters looked mottled. "Oh, wow, he sort of does! Dapples!"

"Brown horses can't have dapples, stupid," said Lisa. "Just dapple gray ones."

"He's not a brown horse, he's a dark chestnut!"

"Same thing," said Lisa scornfully.

"It is not! A dark chestnut—"

They could have argued for a week, but Chickie came home from work and interrupted them. As soon as he had jounced his truck down the lane and brought it to a stop he walked toward them, all his unruly teeth showing in a grin to welcome Lisa.

"Chickie," Rhiannon yelled at him, "Prince's got dapples!"

His grin broadened as he came up and looked. "Yup, them's dapples. Who's your friend?"

Rhiannon made the introduction. Chickie shook Lisa's hand, making it look very small in his big, square grasp. She seemed a little bit afraid of him. "I—I didn't know brown horses could have dapples," she said.

"Chestnut!" complained Ree.

"Any color can have 'em." Chickie turned to Prince and patted him on the neck. "Sign of good health. Tell you what, Ree. Let's put him out with the others a little while, see how they do."

146

"Okay." It was best to do this when Chickie was there to help in case the other horses didn't accept Prince. Their instinct was to drive away a horse that was sick and weak, Chickie had said. That was why he hadn't put Prince in with them before.

Rhiannon turned Prince loose in the big pasture where the other geldings were grazing.

Prince stood still with his head up for a moment, as if he didn't know what to do or think. Then, like a racehorse out of the starting gate, he sprang forward from a standstill into a headlong gallop down the slope.

"Oh, wow!" Lisa exclaimed. But Rhiannon watched with her mouth open, too astonished to speak.

Prince bucked, he kicked, he snorted as he galloped. The other horses scattered from in front of his wild charge and circled around to gallop behind him. The way Prince ran made them look as if they were standing still. They bobbed up and down like puppets while Prince skimmed low to the ground, moving across the pasture like a hawk shadow. Chickie gawked and started laughing.

"Look at him stretch himself!" he yelled, and he laughed out loud like a kid with a gift-wrapped surprise. Then he stopped laughing. "Uh-oh. Get away from the rocks, big fellow."

"Is he going to hurt his hooves?" Ree asked anxiously.

"Hope not."

Without breaking stride, Prince leaped the spread of shelving rock, landing on the grass on top of it. Then he came to a sudden halt and stood tossing his head, king of the mountain. In the hollow below him, the other horses stood staring like the humans. Prince half reared, then neighed, a sound that rang out over woods and pasture and made Rhiannon grab for a fence post as if she needed something to grip.

"He's acting crazy!" she said. Chickie grinned.

"He don't know what to do with himself! He ain't used to feeling good."

"He's pretty," Lisa said.

Chickie told Rhiannon, "You got to remember, we been graining him a lot to get weight on him. Soon as he gets his weight back and we cut his grain, he'll settle down."

Trotting, Prince came down off the rocks. Chickie nodded to himself because the horse was slowing down. "Don't want him to overdo it, though," he said aloud. "Tell you what. I'll feed early, get them all in. You girls keep watching, tell me if he gets himself in trouble." Chickie went into the barn, and Lisa and Ree stayed by the fence.

"He's nice," Lisa said, meaning Chickie.

Rhiannon nodded, eyes on Prince, thinking vaguely about horses and all the things Chickie had taught her and told her. She wished her father would come up to the farm with her. She wondered if her father was like a horse going to the meat auction. Like the diving horse Tiffany, of no use to anybody since his job was gone. They didn't have a farm for steelworkers to go to when the mills closed.

"Lisa," she asked, "what are you going to be once you're done school?"

"Me?" Lisa looked startled, and then her eyes lit up. "I'm gonna be a rock star!" She struck a pose, wrinkled her nose and shrilled out a high note.

Rhiannon shoved at her with the heel of one hand, knocking her out of her pose. "No, I mean really!"

"I really am! I'm gonna be big."

Rolling her eyes, Rhiannon said, "You're gonna be just like my sister!"

"Not me! I ain't getting married until after I'm a star."

Sighing, Rhiannon turned back to the pasture, leaning her elbows on the wooden gate and her chin on her hands. Prince was sniffing noses with some of the other geldings. The horses arched their necks and snorted as they exchanged scent with each other.

"What are you gonna be?" Lisa asked after a minute. She did not sound really interested. What-are-you-going-to-be-when-you-grow-up was a question adults asked when you were in kindergarten, so they could smile when you said something cute.

"I dunno," Ree mumbled. Until recently, she had thought somebody would always take care of her.

Somebody came walking up behind her. "Hi, Bucky!" called Lisa happily, gazing at him.

"Hi, Bucky," said Rhiannon, a lot less happily. She had not seen him since the time he had kissed her and made her mad. She glanced at him uneasily, not sure how to act around him, and he met the glance with a grin a lot like his dad's. Everything's okay, that grin said.

Down in the pasture a horse squealed. Prince and Cameron bumped shoulders and reared, striking lightly at each other with their forefeet. "They're fighting!" Lisa exclaimed.

"They're, like, playing," Bucky said. He leaned on the gate near Rhiannon. "They do that all the time. They fight, but they're really friends. Right, Ree?" He was looking at her with a teasing, big-brother smile on his face, trying to tell her something. It wasn't anything to make her uncomfortable, and Ree smiled back.

"Sure," she said. She and Bucky could be friends.

"You sure they're just playing?" Lisa squeaked.

Rhiannon turned back to the sparring horses and watched with a frown, wondering if she should call Chickie. But he had finished putting the feed in the buckets, and he opened the barn door and rattled a scoop full of oats. Cameron and all the other horses came to attention, then started walking up the slope toward the barn, stopping suspiciously from time to time, as if they thought they were being tricked. They always did that, and they always took their time coming in from pasture. They liked being out. But finally the first one, old deadhead Hoss, reached the barn, and Chickie took him to his stall. Bucky went in to help with the others, and that made Lisa want to go into the barn too, and Rhiannon went along to help and to keep her out of trouble.

"Bucky," Lisa asked him when they were done, "give us a ride home? *Pleeeeease?*"

"I'm not ready to go yet," Ree protested, startled. She was watching Prince eat and scratching his ears from time to time.

"Rhiannon *dragged* me up here to see her horse," Lisa complained to Bucky, pouting.

"He's not my horse. Mr. Miller feeds him and everything." Ree was afraid Chickie would get the wrong idea, hearing Lisa say that. Lisa didn't look around. She was flashing her eyes at Bucky.

"She dragged me through the woods, through briars and stuff," pouted Lisa. "I'm all scratched up and bug bit."

"Well, big whoop!" Rhiannon burst out in disgust. "We can go back down the road, if you're such a—"

"Bucky'll give me a ride," Lisa cut in, speaking to Ree but looking at the boy. "Will you, Bucky?"

"Hey, Bucky!" Chickie hollered from the other end of the barn. "How come she ain't asking me for a ride?"

Bucky pretended he didn't hear. "I'll take you both home when Rhiannon's ready," he said to Lisa. "I got to get my supper yet, anyway." He winked at Rhiannon and went out, strolling up toward the house and whistling.

151

"Good going!" Ree said to Lisa, nasty-nice, because she felt a little mad at her. "Now we don't have to worry about getting home before dark. We can ride Hoss."

Lisa groaned.

Rhiannon enjoyed the evening. She saddled Hoss and rode him and tried to teach Lisa how to ride. Lisa mostly watched and acted bored. The few times she got on Hoss she didn't like the feel of the saddle against her bare legs. Bert gave the girls gobs, rich creme-filled soft chocolate cookies, but Lisa didn't brighten up until Bucky came out at dark to drive them home. Then she lit up like a neon light. "Hi, Bucky!" she exclaimed as if she hadn't seen him for weeks.

Bucky was going to drive them home in his fixed-up, flame-painted Maverick. Rhiannon got in first. She made sure she did, so she would sit in the middle of the front seat and be next to Bucky, just to annoy Lisa. But Lisa didn't seem to mind. All the way home she leaned out of the open car window, waving and yelling hi at everybody she knew, whether it was old people sitting on their porches or kids hanging out on the sidewalks. She wanted the whole world to see that she was riding in a car with Bucky Miller.

"Thanks, Bucky," Lisa enthused when he let them off at the curb near their houses. She stood on the sidewalk and glowed at him.

Rhiannon slammed the car door. Bucky was looking thoughtfully at Lisa. Then he glanced at Ree, smiled and lifted one fist at her, as if she was a guy on his team. Ree waved. Not until after he had driven away did she notice someone else looking at her, someone standing in the dark, narrow yard between her house and the one next door.

"Dad?"

The man turned away and walked off with a hard, angry stride.

Rhiannon went into the house. She heard the sound of somebody crying upstairs. Shawn was standing around just inside the door, looking scared. "Dad hit Deirdre," he said.

"Oh, God," Rhiannon muttered. She wanted to race after her father and bring him back before he got too far away, but she was scared. The mood he was in, he might hit her, too. And upstairs, Deirdre was crying as if she meant it.

Ree ran up the stairs and into her sister's room. Deirdre was sitting on the bed, one hand pressed against the side of her face, crying, not even looking up when Ree stood in front of her. Not even interested in pity. The room was a mess: things thrown around, a lamp smashed on the floor. Rhiannon stooped and pried Dee's hand away from her face. All she saw was a red mark, but she went and shouted down the stairs anyway, "Shawn! Bring some ice!"

"Huh?"

He always said huh, no matter what you asked him to do. Rhiannon felt her fists curl. She felt like hitting somebody herself, but instead she hollered, "Get-a-plastic-bag-put-ice-in-it-bring-it-*here!*"

"Oh."

She knew it would take him awhile. She got a washcloth in the bathroom, ran cold water on it and went back to Deirdre. She sat by her sister and tried to wipe Dee's face.

Deirdre took the washcloth and forcefully blew her nose on it. "Yuck," Rhiannon said.

"Go rinse it, would you?" mumbled her sister.

"Go rinse it yourself."

Deirdre did, then came back to the bed and sat again, sniffling. She had calmed down a lot. Shawn thudded up the stairs, ran in and thrust the bag of ice at her, looking awed. "Did he break your nose or anything?" he asked.

"Shawn, for God's sake," Rhiannon said wearily.

"He just slapped me," said Deirdre in the same tone. She laid the ice against her cheek and held it there.

Ree asked her, "What made him mad?"

"Me, I guess. I told him to go away and let me alone. He came in here and he was just talking and talking at me." Deirdre sounded peevish but subdued. "I told him get lost, and—and—"

Deirdre was stuffing up with tears again. And Shawn was listening, with his eyes wide open.

"Shawn," Rhiannon ordered, "go get the broom and a paper bag and start cleaning up this mess."

"Aw!"

"Do it!"

He went. When he was gone Deirdre said shakily, "I really thought he was going to kill me. But he just slapped me once, and then he started throwing things around, and then he ran out."

"I got to call Mom." Rhiannon got up.

"I guess I deserve it," said Deirdre, and she started to cry again.

Rhiannon looked around at her sister, then went and hugged her around the shoulders, feeling confused, as usual. She knew what had made her father mad. The way Dee had been acting lately was hard to take for long, no matter how understanding you tried to be. Ree was a little mad at Deirdre herself. But . . . She said, "They keep telling us on TV and stuff, nobody's supposed to hit a kid."

"Then how come they do it all the time? In school and everything?"

Rhiannon went and called her mother at work, but it was an hour before Bonnie got home. Her car was gone, and she had walked home alone through the dark streets.

"Call the cops," Rhiannon said.

"I can't. Probably your father is the one who took the car."

"Call the cops anyway."

"And have them looking for your father? What if they find out he hit your sister?"

Bonnie DiAngelo sat at the kitchen table, white-faced, her knuckles in her mouth. She mumbled around her hand, "I'm going to lose my jobs if I keep getting called home from work like this."

Rhiannon wanted to cry, but she felt as if everything would fall apart if she let go even for a minute. She went up to her room and tried to think.

Her father was gone. A runaway. Probably drinking. Maybe he was dead, maybe he had killed himself—no, she wouldn't think that. Maybe he might never come back. Maybe it would be better if he didn't.

No! She didn't want to think that, either.

Her mother wasn't going to call the cops and make him come home. It didn't look as if Bonnie was going to go out and try to find him, either. Rhiannon had seen her mother's face. Bonnie was bone tired. She was doing everything she could already.

Shawn was in his room, probably as scared as Rhiannon. Maybe more scared. He was younger, and he had been home and seen or heard it all. Deirdre was in her messed-up, partly-cleaned-up room, maybe sleeping. Probably not. Mom was downstairs at the table biting her hands. Dad, off somewhere, running away. Each of them in the family, separate. And Rhiannon didn't feel that she could go to any of them. Not strong enough. They would want something from her, and she wanted the same thing herself.

What could she do? Could she go find her father? With the car, he might be anywhere. Pittsburgh, even. Could a friend help her find him? Lisa? Bucky? Chickie? She felt too ashamed for her family to say anything to any of them.

The only one she might be able to talk to was Prince. Her eyes filled at the thought of the horse. He would understand. He had been put alone in a dark place, neglected, starved—for love. . . . He—loved her. . . .

She started silently to cry, her face hidden in her bed. That was what she wanted: love. An always-there love she could depend on, a love that would take care of her and make everything all right for her. But Prince couldn't send her father back to her, and she was scared.

# TWELVE

Very early the next morning, almost before the sky
was light, Rhiannon got up. She had not needed to
set an alarm, because she had barely slept. The night
had been full of confusing thoughts and her own
twitching legs. Morning was a relief. She dressed and
slipped out into the dim hush of dawn, then pedaled
through it as if through a bad dream, down to the old
mine road. She was searching for her father, or
Angel, or both. But she pedaled the length of the
road within the shadowy woods without seeing any
sign of either. No battered Chevy Citation parked at
the gate. No footprints or crescent-moon hoofprints
in the hard, black ground.

She rode back through 27 and up Turkey Ridge
Road to the Miller place. Not even Chickie was up
yet. She hugged Prince and laid her head against his
silky neck, and he rubbed his face up and down her

shirt. But she didn't lean against Prince for long. She straightened up and went to catch a surprised Rowdy. Within a few minutes she had him saddled and bridled and was riding down into the woods. Her lips were pressed tightly together, and she didn't notice how the birds sang or how the deer leaped away in front of her.

She stayed out until the sun was up and the day was starting to get hot. Chickie had already gone to work when she got back. She tended Rowdy, went home, and spent the day doing laundry and keeping an eye on Shawn and Deirdre. Whenever the phone rang she jumped and answered it with shaking hands, hoping and dreading. But there were no calls from her father or about him. When the sun started to go down she went back to the Miller place and rode out again, this time on Butterscotch. Searching.

Not for her father. She knew he was far away. She was searching for Angel.

She hadn't ever gone riding so much, not even before Prince came. For hours at a time, every morning, every evening, she rode, the next day, and the next, and the next. She hardly saw Chickie at all. When she did see him, he watched her with a puzzled frown.

"I never seed you ride so much," he remarked after two days of this.

Ree said, "I'm just looking for Angel." She was tired, and upset by the trouble she wasn't talking about, and she got snippy with him. "That was the whole idea of teaching me to ride, wasn't it? So I could go looking for Angel?"

"Fine with me, sis," Chickie said. "But what are you gonna do with him if you find him?"

Ree looked back at him with her mouth hanging open. She didn't know. In her confused thoughts, or dreams, it seemed to her that if she saw Angel her father would come back, at least for a while. Or in some way things would get better for her, at least for the time being. Anyway, all the horseback riding seemed to help her somehow, if only because she wore herself out enough so that she could sleep at night.

"Like a dog chasing a truck," Chickie grumbled. "Don't know what he'd do with it if he caught it. Well, lookie here." He got a neck lead and showed her how the snap fastened the thick, soft rope around a horse's neck instead of onto a halter. "Might as well carry this with you, just in case."

Ree coiled it and hung it on the saddle. She was starting to have another crazy dream. If she could catch Angel and keep him, would her father come back and stay sober and never go away anymore? If she could have Angel where she could always look at him, would everything always be all right for her?

She didn't see Angel that day. But when she finally went home, after dark, supper was waiting for her in the oven. A neighbor had brought the DiAngelos a huge zucchini, and Deirdre had used cheap imitation cheese to make it into a sort of lasagne. She sat and watched while Rhiannon ate.

"It's not bad," Rhiannon admitted to her.

Deirdre looked awful. She hadn't been washing her hair or using makeup, and her face was puffy and pale, with a fading bruise on one cheek. But she was downstairs, out of her bedroom, puttering around the house and answering the phone when Rhiannon wasn't there. That made Ree feel better about all the time she spent horseback riding. With nobody there to wait on her, Deirdre had to get up and do things for herself.

"Mom finally called the cops," Deirdre said.

Rhiannon stopped chewing.

"Just to ask if Dad was in an accident, or arrested, or like that," Deirdre told her. "And she called all the hospitals. Nothing so far."

Rhiannon started chewing again. Deirdre looked down at the table.

"This is the sort of thing I ran off to get away from," she said.

Rhiannon looked at her and nodded, suddenly understanding. "You thought, like, Keith would make things better for you?"

"Yeah. I thought he would, you know, take care of me and stuff." Deirdre was tracing the flowers on the worn plastic tablecloth with one finger, and tracing around the places patched with tape.

"Like a prince on a white horse," Rhiannon said.

Deirdre stared at her, opened her mouth a couple of times without saying anything, then suddenly started to laugh. It was not a bad laugh, not for Deirdre, even though there were tears hidden in it somewhere. Ree had not heard her sister laugh out loud since before she ran away with Keith.

"Ree, you're something!" Deirdre laughed. "You and your horses!"

Rhiannon sat half annoyed and trying not to smile. Her big sister stopped laughing, reached over and hugged her around the shoulders.

"You and me, sis," Deirdre said with a catch in her voice, "we're just gonna have to take care of ourselves."

She got up and started to clear away dishes, but Rhiannon touched her wrist, stopping her. "What are you going to do, Dee?" she asked. "Really?"

She looked up at Deirdre. Her sister looked back at her.

"I'm going to get my diploma," Deirdre said in a flat voice, "and then, when I can, I'm going to get out of here. I'll take a job in Harrisburg, or Philadelphia, or maybe DC. Anyplace but here."

Deirdre headed out to the kitchen with the dishes. Rhiannon rested her head in her cupped hands. "I wonder where Dad is," she murmured.

Deirdre's voice floated to her hollowly from the kitchen. "Tell you one thing: not on a white horse. That's for sure."

Ree climbed the stairs and fell into bed, and the

next morning at first light of dawn she was out riding again, looking for Angel.

She saw rabbits, and a possum, and a raccoon splashing with its handlike paws at the edge of the creek. She saw a buck deer in velvet antlers, standing and looking at her as she looked at him. She saw the trumpet vine flowers opening. She saw some sort of white bird shining in the sunrise. She did not see Angel that morning, or that evening, or the next day, dawn or dusk.

She rode Punky and Butterscotch and Rowdy and Punky again, and the next morning she rode Hoss.

Riding down through the woods in the half light of very early morning, with the saddle making small sounds to go with the birds in the bushes, with the mist rising off Trout Creek and creeping up the ridge, gray as a dream, until it reached her horse's knees . . . she saw him.

Angel. Like a white ship afloat in the mist, silent, head up, mane and tail stirring like sails, looking at her. And early as it was, feeling as if she was still asleep, or should have been, she silently looked back at him. Or maybe it was because she was so tired, worn out inside, bone tired, like her mother, that she didn't make a sound. Her eyes drank in the sight of him, but her mouth didn't come open and gasp, her head didn't snap up, her hands didn't clutch. And Hoss, being Hoss, plodded along through the woods without changing his pace or so much as twitching an ear.

The white Arabian came toward them at an airy trot, whinnying.

The sound rang out through the woods and echoed back from across the creek. Hoss lifted his head then, in silent, placid interest, and stopped walking, and Angel met him nose to nose, puffing through flared nostrils to greet Hoss in a horse's way. The mist drifted around Hoss's legs, Angel's shoulders.

Rhiannon sat on Hoss without moving, scarcely breathing, just looking at the Arabian. Angel, so beautiful, so—alive. Poised, like a white hawk, ready to fly, muscles moving in his neck and shoulders even though he was standing still. His ears, pricked like wings. And his huge, dark eyes under white lashes. . . . Hair lying so smooth, so white it almost seemed blue, almost seemed to flow like water down his neck, his flanks, then whirlpool and eddy on his chest. Two whorls in the middle of his forehead underneath the tangled forelock that lifted to show them as he tossed his head. That proud Arabian head, blue fire burning deep in the shining eyes. . . . Hoss looked like a lump of dirt next to him.

But Angel liked Hoss. He squealed, sending the long locks of his mane flying, and circled Hoss, sniffing at his hindquarters. Then he stood next to him, pressed up close against him, his shoulder against Rhiannon's knee, and gently he nibbled at Hoss's withers.

With quiet motions, as if it were something she did every day, Rhiannon snapped the lead rope around

Angel's neck. She held the rope with one hand, turned Hoss with the other and rode up the ridge through the mist. It was as if she rode through a good dream or some sort of trance, and as long as she did not speak it would last. It was as if she had captured a unicorn. Happiness would be hers forever. She gazed straight between Hoss's brown ears, not even turning her head to look at Angel, and the Arabian followed along behind her willingly.

They topped the ridge, came out in the sunlight, rode along the pasture fence. The mist floated to treetop level and disappeared, gone in the sunrise.

Chickie was loading a fresh supply of horseshoes into the back of his truck when Rhiannon led Angel around the shed.

"Chickie," she said, very softly.

He turned. His mouth fell open. Hoss, knowing that he was home, stopped walking.

Angel came out of the trance.

Straight up and back he reared, lifting Rhiannon off the saddle by the lead rope gripped in her hand, swinging her around like a toy on a string. Her weight brought him down, and she staggered when her heels hit the ground. Her head spun in bewilderment. What was happening? She was still clutching the neck lead. In fact, she was hanging onto it with both hands.

"Ree! Let go! Don't get yourself hurt trying to hold him!"

She heard Chickie yelling as he ran toward her. He

was not yet close enough to help her. And Angel was plunging, pulling, tearing the skin off her hands with the rope, and any second he could rear and strike at her with his forehooves—

She could get by his shoulder where he couldn't hurt her. She could hold onto him for the few seconds until Chickie got to him, she knew she could. And then she and Chickie between them could put him in a stall, for sure. Keep him forever.

But somehow it wasn't right. Angel was scared, angry, fighting, and . . . and he had been beautiful, like a hope, loose in the hollow. . . .

"Ree! Let go!"

She opened her hands, off balance, falling to the ground, and she heard the hooves drumming. Then Chickie was lifting her up, and she saw Angel flashing away toward the woods, his white mane and tail flying, the lead rope trailing back from his neck and lying along his shoulder, his head thrust high. . . . And then she was crying against Chickie's chest, and his big arms were steadying her against his ample belly.

"It don't matter, Rhiannon!" He was patting her back, his booming voice cutting through her weeping. "Son of a gun, I never thought you'd come nowhere near that horse. I'm a damn fool, I could've got you killed, giving you that rope to bring him in with."

She was crying so hard she couldn't talk, even though it had been a beautiful thing to see Angel sail away beyond the pasture line. Angel belonged free.

"Don't worry about him none." Chickie sounded upset, not about losing Angel again but because she was crying. "He got the halter off, he can get that neck lead off all right. Heck fire, Ree, I don't need him back. Just let him go."

"It's—not—just—that," she managed between sobs. "It's—my father."

She had let something else go when she let go of Angel, and she knew it. She knew she couldn't capture happiness, she couldn't make her father be all right, and—what could she ever depend on completely? Only her own half grown, crying self. Chickie stopped patting her and stood very still. When he spoke his voice was much softer.

"Bucky been telling me things he heard down Hoadley. You been having a rough time, ain't you? But I figured, you don't want to talk about it, I ain't gonna make you."

She cried until she was mostly done, then stepped back from him and nodded, knuckling her eyes. "I got snot on your shirt," she said shakily.

"It don't matter. Horses snot on me all the time."

"Blood, too."

"Huh?" Chickie looked down at the red smears, then at her. "Holy heck!" he burst out when he saw her hands, and he took her by the shoulders and steered her toward the house. "Bert!" he bellowed. "Hey, woman, get the gauze and that there black salve!"

167

The kitchen smelled like bacon and cinnamon buns. Mrs. Miller washed the raw rope burns on Rhiannon's hands, put salve thickly on them and wrapped them in gauze. Chickie hovered, looking as if he wanted to help but didn't know how, until Bert jerked her chin at him and sent him off to work. She sat Rhiannon down at the table and fed her ice cream on hot fresh-cooked waffles for breakfast. The cinnamon buns were for dessert. Ree ate, but she couldn't quite stop crying. Spasms of sobbing kept shaking her from time to time, worse than hiccups that wouldn't quit.

"You get in there on that sofa," Bert told her, "and sleep. You're wore out with misery, is what's the matter with you." She covered Rhiannon with a crocheted blanket.

Somewhat to her own surprise, Rhiannon fell asleep at once. When she awoke, it was early afternoon. She felt odd: calm, and the whole world seemed strange and different. Bert offered her lunch, but Rhiannon shook her head, thanked Mrs. Miller for everything, and went out. She looked at Prince for a while. Down in the pasture with the other geldings, he was still thin, but getting better every day. When he saw her at the fence he whinnied and cantered up to her, but she only said, "Hi, boy." She didn't pat him because of her hands. Then she headed home.

When she got to 27, Shawn met her at the DiAngelo garage. "Dad's back," he said.

 # THIRTEEN

Mr. DiAngelo was on the sofa, still in the same clothes he had been wearing when he left days before, with beard stubble dark on his face, and he smelled of liquor and his own unwashed body. Rhiannon didn't mind barn odors, but she hated that smell. She looked at her father with a hard face. He was lying still, his eyes closed, but he seemed to sense something as Rhiannon stood over him, and with a grimace he opened his eyes. When he saw Rhiannon the grimace turned to a wince of pain.

"Ree," he whispered, "I'm sorry."

She turned away without answering and shouted, "Deirdre!"

"God, don't shout!" her father pleaded from behind her. She didn't look at him. Deirdre appeared on the stairs, holding a tweezers in her hand. She had been shaping her eyebrows, and Rhiannon could see she had washed and curled her hair and put on some makeup. She looked a lot better.

Ree asked her sister, "Did you call Mom?"

"Sure. But she's not coming home. She's afraid she'd lose her job."

"I really thought I could do it on my own," said Bob DiAngelo blurrily from behind Ree. She ignored him.

"You and me got to get him up to the bathtub, then," she told Deirdre.

"You and I," Deirdre corrected. She went to put the tweezers away.

"I made you a promise," Bob DiAngelo said to Rhiannon's back, "and I broke it."

She turned on him angrily. "You sure did!"

"I know I did. Couldn't even keep a promise to my own little girl, and I felt like shit for it." His eyes grew moist. "Had to go places where you couldn't follow me, or—"

"Bull!" Rhiannon scowled at him so fiercely that he stopped talking. "You can shut up about me," she said flatly. "I'm not coming looking for you any-more."

He stared up at her, eyes narrowed against the pain in his head, puzzled. "But, honey, if I can do it for anybody, I can do it for you."

"Not for me, you're not." Rhiannon didn't fully understand why, but since letting go of Angel she knew what she had to do. She had her own growing up to undertake. She couldn't tend to her father's, too. "Come on," she ordered him. Deirdre was standing by her side, and each girl grabbed him by an elbow.

"Wait!" Mr. DiAngelo heaved himself up and sat on the edge of the sofa, his head in his hands. "I can do it myself," he muttered.

"*Sure* you can," said Ree scornfully.

He looked at her, hurt. "I meant getting to the bathroom," he said.

"That's what I meant, too."

He couldn't. They had to help him. "If he pukes on the stairs," Ree said in a hard voice to her sister, "you clean it up."

"*You* clean it up. I'm the one who has to get his clothes off him." Deirdre spoke with bitter humor. "I'm the married woman, right?"

"You both shut up," Bob DiAngelo mumbled. "Just get me into the bathroom, I'll do it myself. Just get me glassa water and some aspirin, wouldja?"

"No," said Rhiannon curtly. "Nobody made you go on a bender. Get it yourself." She left him on the landing outside the bathroom door and went down to the kitchen. Deirdre saw him into the bathroom, then followed.

Rhiannon laid her head down on the table. "He makes me sick," she said to the wall.

Deirdre nodded. "I hope he drowns in the bathtub," she said, sitting across from Ree.

They were quiet. There didn't seem to be much to say. "I like your hair," Rhiannon remarked finally.

171

Her sister was beautiful again, and for once Ree didn't resent it.

"Thanks," said Deirdre. "What happened to your hands?" Rhiannon shook her head against her folded arms. She stayed there, staring at the wall and vaguely thinking, for a long time.

She and Shawn and Deirdre made themselves an early, skimpy supper of canned gravy over bread. Bob DiAngelo didn't want any. After his bath he had gone to bed, leaving his clothes on the bathroom floor. They were so filthy Rhiannon felt like throwing them out, but she put them in the laundry sink to soak. After supper she went out and got her bike.

She passed Lisa walking down street toward Hoadley. Lisa didn't see her, because all the little girls were trailing after her, teasing, and Lisa was ignoring them and everything around her. But Lisa didn't seem mad. She was smiling dreamily. The little girls were chanting:

"Lisa and Bucky sitting in a tree,
K - I - S - S - I - N - G!
First comes love, then comes marriage,
Then comes Lisa with a baby carriage."

Huh, Rhiannon thought, zooming around the corner onto Turkey Ridge Road.

Chickie was at the farm, sending bales of hay up a conveyer belt to Bucky in the loft. It was Saturday, and he had come home early. "How are the hands?" he yelled at Ree above the noise of the conveyer.

"Okay," she yelled back.

Prince was whinnying at her from the pasture fence. She went to pat him, scratching him on the neck with her wrist because she didn't want to use her hand. Then she went back to Chickie. Huge patches of sweat showed on his T-shirt, and the horses really did snot on him all the time and put green slobber on him when they had been eating grass before they nuzzled him. She could see the crusty patches on his shirt and jeans, and she didn't mind them a bit.

"Chickie," she hollered, "can a girl be a farrier?"

He turned off the conveyer so he could hear her better, turning toward her to listen. "What say?"

"Can a girl be a, like, a horseshoer?"

He wiped the sweat off his face with the heel of his hand. "Sure," he said.

"Do you think I could be one?"

He said right away, "You'd probably make a darn good one. The horses like you, for one thing. They trust you. And you're hefty, you'll be strong enough."

"Would you teach me?"

"There you go, Pa," Bucky called from the loft. "There's your future farrier." He was sitting in the hay door and smiling, a nice smile. Ree grinned up at him. She liked him, and she could have him as a friend. She liked Lisa, too, and she could keep being

173

her friend. But she wasn't going to start getting serious about boys. Time enough for that later. Much later.

"There's schools to go to if you want to be good," Chickie said.

Rhiannon felt her grin go away. She didn't know how she was going to have money for school.

"But I can teach you a lot of it." Modestly Chickie spat onto the ground, leaning forward so as to clear his belly. "You want, and if it's okay with your folks, you can start coming with me, watching, handing me things, like that."

"All right!" said Ree eagerly.

"One thing, though." Chickie selected a hay stem from a bale and started chewing on it, leaning against the conveyer. "You might want to think about this. Always aim for the top. The way you was with Prince, taking care of him, I thought many times you ought to be a vet."

"Me?" Rhiannon had never dreamed of it. Being a vet took a lot of schooling.

"Sure. You could be a vet's assistant, start off that way. Earn some money, then go to college. Anybody can see you got lots of brains. You do good in school?"

"Okay, I guess," said Ree doubtfully. She got B's and C's, but her mother and her teachers were always saying she could do better.

"You could work for Doc Shaffer, maybe, in a few years."

"Farriers do lots of vet type things, too," Ree pointed out. "Like treat thrush and abcesses and stuff."

"Sure do. And heck, girl, you don't got to decide today." Chickie grinned and gestured with his piece of hay. "What I mean, helping me would give you a good start on whatever."

Bucky snorted like a horse, then laughed.

"Help you with the hay?" Ree offered.

"Nah. Wait till them hands is better." Chickie turned the conveyer on again, and he and Bucky went back to work.

Ree perched on the wooden pasture gate and stared off uphill, toward the house and driveway. Prince came up behind her and put his head over the gate at her side. Her hands had stopped bothering her, and she patted him without really noticing him while she thought. Things were starting to come into shape for her. She was going to work hard in school and make good grades so she could maybe get some sort of scholarship if she wanted to go to college to be a vet. And Chickie was right: helping him would be a good start. She would learn everything she could about horses from him, and when she was old enough she would maybe go to Hanover where the standardbred farms were and find work until she had enough money to pay her way to school. . . . Or maybe she would go even farther, to Kentucky! Work with thoroughbreds. Maybe she could be a hot walker there, or a groom, or a farrier's assistant, or a vet's assistant, until she got the schooling to be something herself. Maybe . . .

A beat-up Chevy Citation trundled down the lane and pulled up near the barn. Bob DiAngelo got out and came over to where Rhiannon sat on the gate with Prince nuzzling at her shoulder. Ree didn't move when she saw her father, but Prince pricked his ears forward in a friendly way while he studied the new human. Mr. DiAngelo looked pale and wobbly, but he had shaved and put on good clothes, as if he was going to an interview. He stood in front of Ree and didn't try to kid around or get her to say hi to him.

"I called Alcoholics Anonymous," he said.

She just stared at him. He met her eyes steadily, looking cold sober and businesslike.

"I'm on my way to a meeting right now."

"Why are you telling me?" Ree asked, her voice as level as his.

"I just wanted you to know."

"I'd find out soon enough. Why did you come up here?"

"To wish you happy birthday, for one thing."

Ree's mouth jolted open. Her birthday, and she had forgotten all about it, with her father gone. So had everybody else.

"Some birthday I gave you," her father said bitterly.

Ree said nothing. She closed her mouth and looked

steadily at him. After a moment his glance slid away from hers, shifted to Prince.

"Is that the same horse? He looks a lot better now."

"He is." Ree's hand rested on top of Prince's head between his ears, scratching the itchy places where his mane was growing out.

"About time I got up here to see him."

Ree sighed impatiently. She wished he would stop beating on himself. "That's not why you came," she said. "How come you're here? Really."

"I told you! To say happy birthday and tell you I'm going to A.A. It's sort of a birthday present." Her father wasn't businesslike any longer. His voice was shaking.

"Don't pin it on me," Ree told him.

Hurt, and showing it, he said, "I thought you'd at least wish me luck or something."

"But it's up to you, Dad, if you quit drinking."

He stood looking at her with an odd, tight expression on his face. She recognized that look, because she'd seen it on him the day he'd heard her talking about him with Lisa on the phone. Bob DiAngelo had heard the unpleasant truth, and his face showed it. But this time he didn't run away.

Chickie saw him standing in front of his daughter, turned off the conveyer and came over to shake hands.

"Quite a girl you got there, Mr. DiAngelo," he

boomed. "What she done with that horse is really something."

"I'm going to be a vet, Dad," Ree said to her father quietly. "Or a farrier, or something to do with horses."

Bob DiAngelo looked startled. "Any money in that?" he asked Chickie.

"Not around here, there ain't." Chickie grinned, showing all his crooked teeth. "Other places, yeah. Good money."

"Huh." Bob DiAngelo looked at his daughter with a hopeful interest. "Well. I have to get going."

"You meet anybody wants a horse," Chickie said to him, "let me know. I gotta sell some of these."

Rhiannon gasped out loud in dismay. "Not Prince!" she cried.

"Heck, no, Ree! Would I do that? He's your horse."

Bob DiAngelo stood staring from one to the other of them. "How do you figure?" he said without raising his voice. "We can't feed it."

"I feed it and all, but it's her horse just the same. Horse says so." Chickie nodded at Prince. "Look at him."

The gelding was drowsing at the gate with his head lying in Rhiannon's lap and his eyes half closed.

"Huh." Bob DiAngelo looked and actually smiled, a warm, gentle smile. "Well, I have to get a move on. You make sure you get home before dark, Ree."

Walking carefully, not quite steady on his feet, he

got into the car, waved, and slowly drove off. Chickie leaned on the gate by Rhiannon.

"Things better for you now?" he asked after a while.

"Yeah. I guess so. Maybe."

Bucky came out at the barn door, winked at Rhiannon and strolled toward the house. It was suppertime.

"Don't you worry none about your horse," Chickie told her. "I do have to sell a few. Bills getting too high, pasture getting thin. I figure I'll sell Butterscotch, Jingles, maybe Rowdy. Find 'em good homes where they can be out doing things, they'll be better off than loafing around a pasture. Maybe you can help me retrain Cameron and Toby and Shiloh, find them good homes, too. But Prince and the rest of them that needs a home here, they got it as long as I'm Chickie Miller."

Ree nodded. The pasture really was getting to be as much dirt as grass, she noticed. "I think I'll take Prince for a walk," she said.

"Want to come up the house first?"

That was odd. Chickie should have said, "Sure, go ahead." But Rhiannon followed him to the house, and when she saw Chickie's smile, Bucky's teasing grin, and Bert lighting the candles on the cake, she understood. Somebody had remembered her birthday after all. Even Hank was there and helped sing to her.

179

They ate cake and ice cream, then chicken potpie, then more cake. Rhiannon had thought she wasn't hungry, but it turned out that she was. She ate three slices of cake. Bert's cake was even better than her brownies.

And when she came out of the house, Prince was waiting for her at the pasture gate.

She snapped a lead rope to his halter and took him up past the shed, then across the overgrown strip site toward the woods. She walked slowly, full of birthday cake and a quiet no-hurry feeling. When she came to tall yellow flowers covered with tiny yellow butterflies, she stood and looked at them for a while. Farther on, Prince found a patch of clover to graze on, and she stood by him, watching. The sun was warm and as yellow as the flowers. She laid one arm across Prince's back. He was starting to round out, big and sweet and solid. His dark chestnut dapples glowed in the sunset. He lifted his head, and Rhiannon walked him up to the gentle hilltop in the field. Girl and horse stood looking down toward the long shadows of the woods.

Angel came white out of the pine shadow and cantered toward them, the neck lead still trailing from his crest.

The white Arabian, sailing along, skimmed the wildflowers like something with wings. Rhiannon's hands tightened on Prince's lead rope—would the horses fight? But Prince, head up and ears pricked, gave a low-pitched whicker as if greeting an old friend.

Angel slowed to a floating trot. Then the two horses came nose to nose, necks arched so highly that their foreheads almost touched. Their nostrils flared wide with their blowing. Rhiannon stood close to Prince's shoulder, so close that she could touch both horses, but neither of them seemed to know she was there.

Prince was dark and thin, all straight lengths of bone, with the narrow body of a thoroughbred, a lanky neck with the mane lying stubby on it, a straight, narrow head. Angel was summer-cloud white, with the dished face and widest eyes of an Arabian, a curving neck, a graceful, round body and an ever-flying tail. Angel was as wild as wind, and Prince—The chestnut gelding couldn't have been more different. If Prince belonged to Ree the way Chickie said, because he chose, then Angel belonged to no one.

Rhiannon reached out, took hold of the lead rope that dangled from Angel's neck and felt a jolt as every muscle in the Arabian's body bunched to fight her. But her hand had gone straight to the snap. Before Angel could move she slipped the rope off him and away. For a moment, dark eyes full of blue fire looked down on her. Angel snorted softly, then sprang away and ran, his muzzle stirring her hair as he wheeled past her. She watched him plunge back down to the woods and disappear. By her side, Prince watched as quietly as she did, then swung his nose around and nudged her.

"You big baby," she said to him. "I guess you're my birthday present."

It hadn't been a bad birthday after all. Though not even Prince could make everything always right for her. But then, who could expect to catch an angel?

There had been gifts other than Prince, gifts she would keep all her life.

"You want your supper, boy? Let's go on back."

Side by side in the warm sunset light the two of them ambled back to the barn.